VIRUS

STEERN CEWELL

Published by Steern Cewell 2021

ISBN 978-1-5272-9604-6

Book Publishing World
is an imprint of Dolman Scott Ltd
www.dolmanscott.com

CONTENTS

v

CHAPTER 1.

Hi, my name is Stephen, I'm in my 71st year, a statistic I'm not good with. I live on my own, losing my wife to illness in 2014. I'm not good with being on my own, and life is not easy. Mary, my wife, was quite a woman, there was very little in between with Mary, it was either top of the world, or at the bottom of a pit, but I loved her, and miss her daily. The two loves in my life are Paul and Amanda, my son and daughter, if nothing else, those two are my only claim to fame I have left in my life. I still have my Mother going strong, in her ninetyninth year, she's a marvel, not only to survive the virus, but still with most of her faculties. I see her on a regular basis, restrictions are few and far between for the elderly. Denise, my sister, is a few years older than me, and although life is not easy for her, being also on her own, she is well, and we talk most days. Paul, my son has two fine boys, Stephen, the elder, and Nicholas. His wife Jane, is a teacher and a fine mother to my grandchildren. My daughter Amanda, has Andrew, who is grown up, a fine young man. He has a girlfriend, Kim, whom I have yet to meet, other than on line, but she seems like a nice girl. Rog, my daughters husband, is a musician, playing bass in a Pink Floyd tribute band, although performances are now on line, not ideal, but better than nothing.

All the family live in the city, not right in the middle, but a suburb just outside town. Face to face contact is few and far between. This hell has messed up most peoples' lives. I actually live in a little village just outside of Chesterton. It is small, but has everything I need, including an Aldi and a couple of parks that I visit on a regular basis, it's my escape, especially when thing are not going well.

CHAPTER 2.

October 20th 2024. Four years since the virus first struck. It's a different world, such a different world. Why can't they find out how to beat this? Why are these thoughts in my head? It's crazy, it's a dream, just a dream.

Ten to nine, ten minutes to showtime, the daily government do's and don'ts. Same old rubbish, one hundred pound fine for not listening, big brother has us by the short and curlies. As I hook up to channel Dread. I put the kettle on, as usual. It's all getting like groundhog day, still, I shouldn't complain, I have a home, money, and am virus free. "Good morning, the time is nine o'clock", blurts from the radio as I pour myself a coffee. "Your government continues to keep you safe", going on to another thirty eight deaths, believe that if you can. Same old rubbish, talking themselves up, still the area forecast has to be listened to, where we can and can't go, to be in a no go area will cost you one hundred pounds for first offence, ten percent of your worth 2nd offence, and the prisons are full of third offenders. Technology helps, for those who can afford it, with the app. warning of entering a no go zone. Today is my designated shopping day, an hour to sort food and essentials to get me through the week. This week I have the one to two time slot at Aldi's, the only shop now, apart from chemists, all other stores taken over by Aldi, with government backing, with most of the government cabinet share holders. "Have a great day, and stay safe", heralds the end of the news.

With nothing to listen to, my thoughts again turn to that weird dream, nightmare? No, it wasn't frightening, but so real. I can remember every second of it, like no other dream I've ever had. It's repeated itself three nights running. Dreams can be so real, we all have them, but these, they're different, like someone ringing me up and telling me stuff. I've probably been in this horror far too long. I finish my coffee and head for the bathroom, ordering some soft rock from Alexa, keeping some amount of noise in the background, I'm not good with silence, but if I'm honest, this time it's to keep the dream away. I turn on the shower, checking the water with my hand. The first step in takes my breath away. I've never really enjoyed showers, and I'm in and out as quickly as I can. It's quarter to ten as I enter the lounge, and settle myself on the sofa. Picking up a pad and pen from the table to make my shopping list, skipping Bat out of Hell by Meatloaf with Alexa. Then, as I start my list, shutting my eyes to think, I begin to feel strange, the shopping list melts away from my mind, and all I can see is that dream.

CHAPTER 3.

I try to open my eyes, they flicker between open and shut. I can't do anything about it, all I can see is that dream. I can't open my eyes now, I feel my heart racing. I'm awake but dreaming, is the only way I can explain it. I see myself being filmed, I'm standing still as the camera zooms in towards me, nearer and nearer until I can't make anything out, and then enters me, inside me, I still can't move. I try to resist the dream, I know I'm awake, but there's nothing I can do. The camera continues through my body. Suddenly I can see shapes, I'm not near enough to make them out. Tiny specks speeding round. I squint, trying to make out the figures. I can make them out now, they're people, millions of them, all doing the same thing, going the same way. The camera is still now, focused on the people, and then as soon as this crazy dream started it ends.

I open my eyes expecting to see something changed, but it's all the same. What the hell is happening to me. I'm there on the sofa, in a daze for ages. I take several deep breaths to bring me back to some sort of normality, and eventually I begin to focus on the shopping list.

We've been in this nightmare for over four years, steadily getting a grip on controlling the virus during the summer months, only to be hit by new outbreaks as the virus mutates as winter arrives, each time it's more severe than the last time, killing millions. Africa has been decimated with over twenty one million dead. I suppose we should be thankful we have had only half a million deaths, Thankful!!!. What a mess!

I sort through the cupboards, adding things to my list, although to be honest, nothing much changes, same old, same old. Ok, just a matter of waiting for one o'clock. I pick up my guitar and strum a few chords, but my heart is not in it. Gone is the excitement of a new riff, a new song. What's the point I think as I return to the kitchen, and the kettle, I'm drinking far too much coffee. I take my drink and sit down on the sofa, I sip my coffee, and relax into my seat. I know what's coming, but something inside me has to know.

CHAPTER 4.

Almost immediately I'm there, watching millions of tiny people rush around. I need to know what they're doing, and why. As I look closer, I can see there's not one, but two lines, one red, one green, and now I can see they're going in opposite directions. Suddenly I'm catapulted at incredible speed into one of the lines, coming to a shuddering stop. All I see now is a bright flashing light, on off, on off, but different, more like a pulse, Yes, that's what it is. What am I seeing, am I watching my heart beat? It's all around me. The beat is fast, I check my pulse, counting the beats, but I know what that tells me, they're the same. I'm inside my body, watching my heart beating. As I listen to it, a calm begins to flood over me, and I'm at peace, watching, listening. Then, as if purposely pulling me away from this peace, I'm catapulted back to reality, and I'm unsure exactly where I would rather be. I try to pick up the thread of the dream, but it's gone. I really don't know how to react. What the hell is going on, and what I need to do. And of course, why me?

It's time to get myself to Aldi, really the last thing I want to do, but I can't afford to miss my slot. As I leave the flat, putting on my mask, I lock up and walk to the car. First job is to ring my mother, she answers in her usual upbeat manner. She been imprisoned for over four years in her flat.

Myself and my sister get her out during the good weather to parks and such, but there's very little contact with the rest of the family. In her ninety ninth year, she's a marvel. The rules for the over seventy five year olds are few and far between now, but together, the three of us agree to continue a safe way of life for her, and we believe that it has kept the virus from her. She relays her shopping list and I set off to Aldi's. I join a small queue of cars at my local Aldi, number plate recognition allow cars to enter the car park. Mask back on I stretch a pair of latex gloves on and remove a trolley from its housing. I must admit to the fact that this hour has become something to look forward to, I'm out of the flat, and although I can't meet anyone, being around people has a good vibe for me. I take a scanner from the sterile cradle. It's one way round the store so I have to be careful I don't miss anything, there's no going back, I take up much of my hour missing nothing. I enter the payment area and point the scanner at the till to pay. Having loaded the shopping into my car boot I return the trolley to the used bay. I leave the car park and join the petrol queue and eventually pull alongside a spare pump. I put on another pair of gloves and begin to deliver my three gallons of petrol, my weekly limit. Technology assists me from having to pay by card and I'm back behind the wheel and head home.

Home again, and the weekly headache of de bugging the shopping, spraying each sealed unit before storing them in cupboards and fridge. I make a note of mam's stuff so as not to forget anything when I take them to her tomorrow. By the time I've finished it's close to four o'clock and realizing I've had nothing to eat I open a slab of cheese to make a sandwich, put on the kettle and make a drink, grab a packet of crisps and settle down onto the settee. I open my iPad and engross myself in what sport there has been and news. I'm finding it difficult to concentrate, but I refuse to close my eyes and relax.

I finally get into the football news when the tone of my iPad tells me I have a new message, I click on to messages. My heart begins to pound as I see to my horror, two figures, one red, one green. I take my iPad from my lap and throw it onto the settee next to me. I jump up, I can hardly move with fear. Not daring to even look at the iPad I sit down on a rigid black chair, trying to calm down. I look over to the iPad. "This can't be happening". For a few moments more I don't move. Eventually I rise, and walk, with purpose and no little amount of anger and pick up the iPad expecting to see what had left me in such a state, but there's nothing. I quickly click on "Last message", it's blank, no red or green figures. Wait, heading the blankness is "Stephen, for you". "Who are you?" I text back, and the whoosh of the iPad tells me it had gone. But where?.

Before I know, it's late, and time for sleep. I'm torn between wanting more of this strangeness, and needing to sleep. I still take drugs at night, so even if I wanted to stay awake for any length of time I couldn't. I settle down on the sofa, watching an episode of Morse, and although I've seen it times before the familiarity is comforting. It's got to be the norm for me, I drop off on the sofa, wake after a while, then trundle off to bed. Eventually I drop off.

I wake with a start, and look at the clock, it's quarter past two, I've been asleep for three hours, and no dreams. I'm bulled by that and feel calm as I make my way to the bedroom and into bed. As I lie there waiting for sleep I hear a creak, a noise, something. I listen intently. Eventually I have to leave my bed to check round the flat. Nothing, no one. I climb back into bed. I plump up my pillow with a few fist pumps, When!!! "Stephen, for you", rings out, and before I can think, I'm catapulted into another unbelievable state. This time I'm standing in between the red and green lines, in front of a mirror, it has to be a mirror because I'm face to face with myself. "For you", comes from the mirror. "What's happening?", rolls from my lips,

V

my movement mirrored by the image in front of me. "You know", I close my eyes, trying to access my thoughts away from this madness. "I don't, do you want me to do something?" I scream, but there's nothing. My eyes catch sight of the eyes in the mirror, they're troubled. It's thinking, and after a short pause, "To Understand", becomes the last contact of the night before I'm returned to normal. Normal? It's anything but normal. I lie there for a while going over what had happened, but sleep gets the better of me, and the day is done.

CHAPTER 5.

I wake about seven thirty and drag myself into the bathroom for a wee. Still tired I slipped back into bed, and by no time at all it's quarter to nine, and after lying there for a while, I get out of bed. I can't be bothered to shower, so I just swill my face and clean my teeth. First job, kettle on. Not wanting to watch the kettle, I moved into the lounge and sink into the sofa. Mornings are not my best time of the day. Hearing the kettle click, I'm up pouring my coffee. As time passes I start to come around and my mind turns to the messages, the mirror. As I try to remember exactly what was said, I realize that the voice I heard, was mine. Is it just a dream? I start to think again. I text around the family, hoping they're all well, something I do most days. I have learned not to expect an immediate reply back, Amanda can sleep for Britain, and Paul's not one to check his phone. I start to think about what is happening, and I realize that I'm being drawn in, wanting an answer to what it means. So I close my eyes, not to sleep, but connect to what? I'll give it a name, "V" for Virus, yes, that's good, after all he has entered my body like a virus. "V" I cry, as If I'm summoning a spirit, I smile to myself. "Come on out," I screech, it seems it's not listening. I open my eyes and give them a rub then set about giving the flat the once over with a dust cloth and Hoover.

Life in 2024, where to start, probably with the virus, after all it's where it all started. I'm talking early 2020 when the virus first struck, and all countries failed to work together, allowing it to spread uncontrolled, no more so than the UK, where a totally inept government failed in almost every area of fighting the virus. I think the overwhelming thoughts were, that it would be ok when we get the vaccine, maybe If that was all we had to do we may not be in this mess today. During the winter of 2021 the virus took hold again, and this time no matter what we did, we couldn't stop it. it all began to look like an apocalypse. Another black death, but worse, and no longer was the government looking to control the virus, but beginning to control what it could, US. That was when the government, and the rich, took control. No longer asking us to do things, but telling us, with punishment for breaking the rules. As time went by more and more rules were imposed on the population and a state of dictatorship began. Some argue that it was the only way, and for some it was, mainly the haves, who were equipped with PPE and could guard against the virus but it was the have nots it hit. The first wave, in the winter of twenty twenty, killed over three million, since when there's been seventy four million deaths. Admittedly, deaths have been reduced significantly as people are kept apart, that's ok for countries like Britain, but the third world countries it's impossible, millions are dying. As for myself, mom who I visit once a week plus drop off her food and medicines. The rest of my family's life is all online. Mobile phones have become trackers. The government makes sure everyone over seven has a phone. Anyone outside must have their phone with them, and have the 'Stay Safe' app. This is the government's app, Anyone caught without the phone whilst out side, would face fines for the first time offenders and up to a prison stay for re offenders.

I'm up onto my exercise bike, my daily routine. I don't want to, but needs must. As I pedal steadily, I find myself listening to the click that counts each cycle. I'm drawn into the beat, and as it reaches that of my beating heart I'm again locked into V's grip. My eyes shut I see the pulsing of my heart. I continue pedalling, waiting for contact from V. Although not in control, I'm pretty calm even though I know he's coming. Then, "You are chosen", rings into my ears, my voice, but not me. I wonder whether to ask questions, or just wait and listen "We must reduce", is the next to come from V. Uncontrollably I ask "Reduce what?" That brings silence, somehow I know he's thinking of his reply, but as he's thinking the beat begins to increase, and soon reaches alarming speed, faster and faster I pedal, my legs a blur. "You", booms out. With that, V has gone. I suddenly realize the speed that I'm pedalling, I simply couldn't pedal this fast for ten seconds, let alone for the time I have. I'm not out of breath, not a bit. I begin to slow down, and stop. I just sit there, numb, trying to make sense of what has just happened. I recount what V had said. "We must reduce." I have to wait a while before I can go onto V's answer to my question. I berate myself for asking. Stupid, I know to ask questions could only make things worse. "You!!!" "Me? Reduce me?". This can't be real, what's happening to me, it's madness, is it my madness?.

CHAPTER 6.

I check my free hours as we're given four hours per week where we can be outside. I usually walk round the local park, and I was desperate to get out before I totally lose it. Seeing I still had over three hours remaining. I quickly check the areas I can visit, and as usual Bouskell park was one. I hastily grab my jacket and put on a mask. A beep from my phone, as I leave the flat, tells me I'm now using my free time.

I set off to the park, which is just five minutes or so from the flat. It's cold but dry and there's glimpses of the sun that makes it easier. As I begin my walk I think to myself, don't let this thing take over your life. I have a family, and to lose them again I couldn't bear. My daughter was diagnosed with M E before the virus struck. Apart from missing the contact of loved ones, working from home suited her down to the ground. My son is a key worker, on the railways, based in Derby, keeping what's left of the railway going. Then there's mam aged ninety nine with all her faculties, dealing with the pandemic brilliantly, even though we know that the government's policy of removing all restrictions, stating they should be allowed to enjoy there latter years, but everyone knows that it's a form of euthanasia. The population of over eighties has fallen from four percent, to one percent.

My walk is slow, gone are the days of power walks, and my head begins to clear. My thoughts turn to my own health problems, with depression littering my life, eventually leading to a four month stay in a psychiatric hospital, so any idea of discussing this madness with someone would be a complete no no. Even coming from a normal person it would sound crazy. I begin to think about V again. It's not going away, I can't control it, so I'm steadily realizing I have to face it. I don't have a choice.

So how do I manage this? V is telling me that I'm the problem, or that's the way I read it. That's scary, frightening, and I am afraid. It seems I have done something wrong, but what. It's pretty clear, or as clear as it can be, that contacting me isn't easy for V. It's like he's having to learn how to say what he wants. I feel that I'm still in control of my thoughts when V isn't there. I don't understand why I'm seeing inside me, seeing my heartbeat, and the lines of people racing around. And now the exercise bike, just thinking about it, the speed, I simply could never physically do that. So, V can not only show me things, he can also control me physically. I came off that bike breathing normally. I come to where I started at the park, and walk home. As I enter the flat I check how much free time I have remaining. As I enter my lounge, my gaze goes straight to the bike, I think about getting on it again but I couldn't deal with anything else at the moment.

Having missed breakfast, I butter a couple of rounds of bread and make a ham and cheese sandwich. Not fancying a hot drink I pour myself some squash, grab a bag of crisps and settle down onto the sofa. I pick up my iPad thinking maybe there's some help out there, I begin putting in what had happened. This is not a good idea, the first comment comes from Mark, get this, Mark Mars. He starts with how many times he has been abducted, taken to Mars, and injected with something that gives him superpowers. Don't think I'll reply, probably have to block this nutcase. Listen to me!!!, if what I'm saying doesn't sound like the ramblings of a complete nutter. Green and red people inside my body, crazy. I enter into Google and a whole load of medical stuff about green skin comes up. No answer here then.

I finish my lunch and flick through the tv trying to find something to watch, as always I end up with channel ten, and an episode of Lewis, followed by Heartbeat, maybe the location of both programmes are the attraction, Mary and I loved Oxford, and the memory of a trip to Heartbeat country with her and my mother is fondly remembered. This getting old isn't fun. My eyes begin to close, it's hard sitting for long periods nowadays, without dropping off, so I quickly jump up and pick up my guitar and begin to play 'Fear', very apt.

I pull the window to and close the curtains as day turns to night. I don't know what to expect, I only know something will happen. I move to the kitchen and start washing up. Normally I would leave it till the morning, but I'm desperate for something to do. I wonder if I shouldn't take my anti depressant medication, just incase they have some bearing on what's happening, but I know if I don't I won't sleep. As usual I start snacking on crisps, yogurt, ice cream, whatever I have in. They call it comfort eating, but I don't feel comforted, just podged. I decide it's time for bed. I take my iPad and phone that's fully charged to do some recording, maybe if I had something recorded, it would make it easier to decide whether V is real, or I'm totally mad.

I settle down to yet another episode of Lewis, although I've seen every episode time and time again, I've no idea who's the murderer this time. Generally I have the tv on for background noise as I surf the net. I decided that I shall start recording when Lewis has finished, so I need to stay awake till then.

Eleven, I start recording. I'd forced myself to watch Lewis till the end, even though I remember who did it half way through, I'm tired, the drugs make me so, but I'm far too uptight to relax to sleep. My thoughts kick in, thinking maybe I can't start a conversation with V, and simply have to wait until he's ready, and tonight will be a damp squid. Thoughts run through my head as the minutes pass. Suddenly!!! My body, uncontrollably empties my lungs of air and I find myself gasping. I try to reach for my phone to get help, but the further I reach for it, the further away it gets. The clock on my bedside table tells me it's two forty seven. Before I could go through my thought process, I'm hit with a terrible screeching noise of different pitch. It's almost unbearable, my head feels like it's about to explode. Finally I'm allowed to take a long breath in, that enables me to realize what I'm hearing. It's not some random noise but the screams of thousands of people, those people, inside me. And as soon as that thought enters my head, I'm rushed to the front of the mirror, that mirror. V has me. I can't fight it, and to be honest, I don't want to. The screams begin to subside, familiar sights appear, red and green pulsing light, my heartbeat. I turn my head to the mirror and my reflection. I'm waiting, eyes fixed on my reflection. As I stand there I begin to calm down, as if V is keeping me safe. V is in complete control at this point, as if he needed to keep my body in a relaxed state. My image suddenly blurs like water rippling my image. Then!!!, "I am learning. it is not easy for me, you must know. What, what do I have to know?" speeds without thought from my lips heralding terrifying tortured screams, red and green faces surrounding me. I dare not move, I can't move. As the faces withdraw and the screams fade away, "I need you, I am where I have not been before, you must save me, save yourself." I don't know what to think, but I need to ask if V wants to hurt me. This question causes madness within the red and green ranks, as they're turning each an every way, they're not screaming but like chattering, they're communicating with each other, I guess they're working out an answer to my question. The chatter stops and they move back into lines. "No!!!". Something makes me turn from the mirror, and when I look back there's nothing, just the darkness of my bedroom, V has gone. I lie they're for a while, then I sit up. I grab the bedside light and illuminate the bedroom. Somehow I know V won't be back tonight. I look at the clock 2.47. I pick up my phone and press play, in hope more than anything, and as expected, nothing. I get out of bed and go for a wee,

wasting no time or thought I quickly get
back into bed, and to sleep.

CHAPTER 7.

I wake at eight, refreshed, like nothing has happened. I pick up my mobile and quickly start to relay what I can remember of V's visit. Hoping that I leave nothing out, with most mornings being a pretty awful part of the day for me it's not easy. I should get in the shower, but can't be bothered, so I head for the kitchen for caffeine. I don't know if it's the same for you, but that first boil of water seems to take twice as long as any other part of the day. I take my drink and move to the sofa. I glance at the exercise bike, remembering the unbelievable speed I generated. I'm tapping at my phone as I sit down, and account that moment.

Normally the old memory doesn't work that well now days, but it's as if I can just bring up every word, every moment of V's visit. First there was that dream, three consecutive nights. In it I would be sitting looking at the horizon. I was somehow lifted and taken on a journey. What comes to mind is that character from Baghdad, on the carpet. I was flying with the birds, well that's how it seemed. I wasn't scared, I know that's V's doing, heights terrify me. My view wasn't up, but down and what was underneath me. I'm travelling over Oceans, countries, continents, over mountains as if I was circling the whole planet, finishing back where I started. And that was it. Three nights exactly the same.

Now I'm not a believer in ghosts, and all that stuff, but I can't deny my thoughts were being pushed towards the afterlife. Something or someone is trying to contact me. Of course, my thoughts turn to my late wife. It would be easy to think that she was trying to contact me, after all, many times have I hoped it could happen, but I can't tie anything about our life together with V, although she loved to travel, maybe the dream? I know I'm fooling myself but it doesn't hurt anyone.

V, needs to contact me, he, she, it, has made that clear. He's singled me out, as to the reason why. I ask questions and am fearful of the answers. I seem to be causing V fear linked to death, not just V's, but mine too. But of course, there is another route I can take, I'm going mad. By this time my thoughts are so overwhelming

I need to stop, for my own sanity. I decide to shower, hopefully taking my mind off it. As I shower, touching the cold side, I gasp, bringing bad memories of showering in the mental health unit I spent four desperate months in. I'm glad to say these days I rarely dwell on that time, but with all this going on my thoughts are hyper sensitive.

CHAPTER 8.

A new day begins with the usual reluctance to leave my bed. I'm very much on autopilot, kettle on, bathroom, coffee and sofa. Today I plan on a visit to my mother's. It's been a while since I spent time with her other than delivering shopping or medications. The restrictions imposed by the government give over seventy fives exemption from almost all of them, you know my views on why. However my sister and I keep contact to a minimum, making sure she is kept safe, regardless of the government's attempts at eradicating the elderly.

As I get myself together, listening to the government's daily crap, I can't help but wonder when my next visit from V will take place. It seems that night time is favoured by V. I don't know why, but I seem to believe V is protecting me somehow. Contacting me at night only gives me the day to do the normal stuff, and if I can be confident there'll be no contact during the day, that would be most welcome. My state of mind is pretty delicate. The weather looks ok as I leave the flat and head to the car park. I throw my bag of rubbish into the communal bin, taking care not to touch anything. I pump a few drops of sanitizer into my hands just to make sure, and set off to mothers. The usual queues stretch from Aldi's doorway, the two metre distancing being more than adhered to as fearful shoppers-inch slowly forward. The drive to mam's takes about a quarter of an hour. There's not much traffic, most having already travelled to their work place. There's the usual splattering of joggers, but very little else. I pull into mam's car park, and put on gloves and mask. We greet each other fervently, visitors are always welcome, despite the virus. I sit myself down and begin to chat. There's no post to sort out, so, "Tea?" I head to the kitchen and make the brew, taking two cups from her cupboard and place them in the sink ready to sterilize them with boiling water. Mam like her tea really weak, basically you just have to show the teabag to the water. I spend half an hour or so chatting. My mother is a remarkable lady. She has adapted to the new way of life, accepting the limitations that the virus has made. Although it took a while, she has a good grasp on technology, and for a ninety nine year old is remarkable. The kids and grandchildren keep in regular contact with her. My sister Denise, lives a couple of minutes away, but despite that, visits only occasionally, something that the three of us have agreed on, to keep her safe, despite the government. We say our goodbyes with the virtual hug.

As I leave the flat I sanitize all the surfaces I have touched. I remove my gloves and mask, again sanitize my hands, and set off home. I'm home in no time and as I enter the flat the usual beeps come from my phone as it connects to my wi fi, also there's the melodic sound of my WhatsApp messenger ringing out. I sit to see who's messaged me. It's not the kids. Immediately my mind goes into overdrive.

Were my thoughts of V leaving my days free wrong? I must have sat there for a couple of minutes before I click on the WhatsApp symbol. All that's there is "Eleven". It seems I have got it right, and now I know that V is actually listening to my thoughts, he knew my thoughts, and has answered them. I put my phone down and pick up my iPad to put the latest message from V down, but actually, I really don't need to. The fact is that I can remember every word, thought, action, as if just happened. I believe I'm getting to know V's mind. There I go again, believing he's real, not just my imagination, and it looks like I'm leaning heavily on V being male.

CHAPTER 9.

So, as afternoon ends and the evening draws in, it looks like I have my first, appointment with V. I'm trying to be positive by this new revelation, but to be honest I've been stressed ever since he told me about eleven o'clock, and I'm sure that will get worse the nearer it gets. I try to get into an old black and white war film that I haven't seen for a while, but it's mainly just background noise. Mostly I'm tapping away at my iPad. Technology is pretty much everything these days as we live in this new virtual world. To be honest,

I'm better equipped than most with the lack of physical contact. Yes, ok, I miss Mary terribly, but I've never been a people person. I simply don't fit in, being always the quiet one of a crowd. It's always been like that. When I was in my teens I can remember many times when people have commented on me having little to say. I'm one of those souls who has all the answers, words, charisma, but inside my head only, it's when I open my mouth that it all goes wrong.

The time draws ever closer to eleven. I've taken my medication at the normal time and beginning to regret it as it begins to take hold. I get up and grab a few biscuits, but they're gone in a flash and I'm back fighting sleep. My mind begins to meander in that half asleep, half awake stage, to past memories I'd rather not visit. Is this sleep?. I open my eyes as if to wake. What the!!!. There in front of me is a big glass box. I can't make out what it is, but I'm walking towards it. I see it's moving as I get nearer to it, it can't be surely. It is, it's a cable car, there's no cable but I'm sure that's what it is. I hate cable cars, but can't stop myself from getting ever closer to it. As I move up to it the door opens and I step inside. I scream inside, trying to wake myself up. It's a nightmare. The car brushes foliage before heading towards the heights that terrify me so. I can't move with fear. How can I have been so wrong about V. Then to my horror, the top of the car begins to disappear, like the car is being rubbed out around me. All I can see is the miles underneath me. I cling to what is left of the car, screaming as the wind sways the car viciously left and right. My legs hammer against metal rails either side of the doorway. As the car slowly fades away, my grip loosens. I can no longer hold on. I see the ground far below me and my fear takes away my screams, and I'm falling. I close my eyes, I realize that V is here to take my life, after all he had held me responsible, but for what, I'll never know. It seems like I'm falling forever when my eyes open. I instinctively turn my head and see my bedside clock. I let out a loud expletive, "You Bastard", follows at the top of my voice. It seems I can't separate between real, V and dreams. I've had similar dreams, falling, we've all had them, but because of V, everything is screwed up.

I gradually come round, I smile, "Just a bloody dream", I'm drenched in sweat, totally shattered from the experience. I have to lie there for some time before

I leave my bedroom to make myself a cuppa. I decide to shower after my coffee. I peer at the weather, then settle onto the sofa to have my drink. I recap the nightmare. God, am I screwed up. I decide to carry out my plans of a shower and begin to run the water, testing the temperature with my hand before stepping in. As I said, showers are not my favourite washing technique, but they're quicker. I pour some shower gel onto the flannel and begin washing. My eyes close to prevent them stinging from any soap I may get in them while I washing my top half. I rinse off and move to the nether regions. O my God!!!, My legs, on each side of them are several blue black bruises. It's difficult to comprehend what's happening to me, and why. Could this be a mental illness, I've seen what schizophrenia is from my time in hospital, and the bruises, did I do them myself?. As I look closer at the bruises, I remember the two metal rails that my legs were ramming against, and sure enough my bruises matched them perfectly. I'm so confused. Other than trying, and succeeding in totally terrifying me, I can't see any positives that V has gained. I contemplate calling my doctor's surgery, but me and doctors never work. My experience of being with and watching, unable to do anything to help my Mary, had done for me where doctors were involved. But I know I must go on, I can't give up, but maybe I do need-help.

Once again, as if listening to my thoughts, V responds. "Our ways are limited by your thoughts, we are not totally in control of our response". I'm glad of that, although I'm even more confused, but V is learning, becoming more able to understand. There seems little doubt V is becoming more fluent in his communication, learning? Yes. But I still don't know why me. I do know that I'm really struggling to cope with it all. How much more can I take.

All this has bought me to midday. I think about a walk on the park, but I'm shattered. Everything goes round and round my head. The dreams, V, trying to make sense of it all. One moment he seemingly is protecting me, then the next he's almost terrifying me to death. I hurry through what I know about V. Firstly there's the dreams, so vivid, incredibly, they put me inside myself. And V's apparent reason for blaming me, for causing his fear. Why does he hold me responsible. It seems strange that if I am responsible for all these things affecting V, and he can do the things he has shown me, why I'm still here, alive. Maybe he can't actually hurt me, not physically anyway, but I have the bruises, they're real, I can see them, they hurt. I do nothing for the rest of the day. I need to rest.

(9a)

"I'm a bit of an hypochondriac" I fear death, I always have done. I was having tests, believing I had that illness. Just the word disturbs me. I turned to drink, with vodka being my choice of poison. Each morning was a quick, panicked dash to the local shop for a quart bottle. Three large glasses with coke was enough to knock me out with enough left to do the same when I woke. I was under a psychiatrist, having a CPN, (community psychiatric nurse). Eventually they decided a spell in the local mental health hospital would be advisable. At the time I didn't resist, but that's where my problems grew and took hold. The amount of abuse , targeted at the most vulnerable was nobody's business. Each week we would be ushered into a room to face four or five medical staff, each one picking at your brain. The whole thing was terrifying. Three times a day we would queue for medication, as if we were cattle to be herded. And then the regular siren would bring staff running to corner a patient who was not biding by the rules, and jab them, leaving them in a state of sedation for the rest of the day. The doctors, who mainly were having their six months working with people with mental health issues. We were like guinea pigs to them. Then there were the patients themselves, and abuse between them, between me, using me then turning away from the hell they caused, with the staff doing nothing to prevent it. Night time saw the heavies come on. Big black men, who hadn't the slightest knowledge of how to deal with mental health. Having to ask them for a sandwich or biscuits that were stored, for patients, in a locked room. They would eventually prize themselves from their chair, and saunter over with a look of bloody hell written across their face. Most had limited use of English. My weakness was picked up on and used while the staff looked on. It was four months of my life I prefer to forget. not least of all for the stress and hurt I put on my family. I'm back in the lounge now, and put on the box, taking my mind away from the past, after all, I must concentrate on the future, and what's next from V.

CHAPTER 10.

After a few hours of basically doing nothing, I decide to give the family a quick hello. I ring mam and my sister, they're both ok, as are Amanda and Paul. It gives me a lift to know that all's well with them. I lift myself from the sofa and draw the curtains as the light begins to dim outside. Days seem to fly by, mainly because all I seem to be doing is dealing with V's effect on me. Even now, at eight o'clock I'm thinking of tonight's encounter. I'm struggling to understand why I'm not terrified, but I'm not.

The usual stuff is on the tv, it's just background noise as I search for sports news on my iPad. It's almost impossible to concentrate fully on anything. Checking the phone regularly tells me where my mind is. Before I know it it's ten o'clock, I'm generally in bed at this time, finding the comfort of the bed more relaxing, and with the tv in there, why not. For a change I have the news on, it's not for the faint hearted. The vast number of deaths brings a sombre moment that I could do without, you see why I rarely watch the news. Seventy millions deaths is the new total. The amount of people over seventy has dropped worldwide from seven percent to two percent. It's generally held that the virus was being used by governments. Euthanasia is what many countries people cry. It does seem strange that most of the western world has less restrictions for the over seventies. I begin to feel the effects of my medication, so I turn the tv onto a Midsummer murder that has just started.

I find it difficult to relax to sleep, even with my medication. That's not wholly to do with V. I've always found it difficult to empty my mind. Yoga and the likes never did anything for me, and when your depression becomes bad enough to hospitalize you, I can assure you that it's rammed down your throat. So generally I just drop off mid thought. Of course V has made it almost impossible to relax at anytime. And as if to prove a point, a new thought enters my head. Why did I call this thing V. The answer of course, V for virus, but why have I linked this thing to the virus. I'm too tired to go through all the contact I've had from V, and right now I can't link V with the virus. I eventually drift off, although

I no longer seem to know the difference between asleep and awake. The dream are now as real to me as when I'm awake. I find I can now carry a thought I have when awake, into my dreams, carrying on the thought without tiredness taking over. Ok, so maybe I've wrongly linked V to the virus. Is there anything that has happened to do with the virus, I can't think of anything. My dream moves to re naming V, but I can't recall how that ended up. The virus has been with us over four years, so why now? Why not before. The more I seem to dig into it, the more confused I get. But I have to admit, I may have got it wrong. The night seemed too full of those thoughts, those dreams, and nothing much else, as if I may have hit something important. I didn't feel that V was there. No messages, indeed it felt like a normal night, with normal dreams. And as I wake it's clear V hadn't been with me for the first time since it all began. You may think it would be normal for me to have my hopes raised of an end to all this, but I knew that wasn't the case, and V will be back.

I feel relieved and rested as I leave the bedroom. I click the kettle on as downstair's dog begins to yap, no doubt to go out and do his business, so I'm told. To be fair, mornings are the only time I hear her. It's not a sound heard that often anymore, since the fake news that the virus was 'carried by animals' hit just over a year ago, causing a world wide cull of pets. Even in Britain people were having their pets put down, and there was mass hysteria in other countries, leading to horrifying scenes everywhere. Who started it all is still unknown, but to this day, there's still an uneasy acceptance around pets. I catch up with the news as the daily report starts. Very little changes, but it's Sod's law if I give it a miss there would be something that costs me. My weekly free time re sets itself, there's no carry over of unused time, so I try to make sure of using all my time each week.

I don't know why, but I still set down everything to do with V, as I said, I can still bring them all up in my mind as if it had just happened. I eventually get round to opening the curtains to a bright new morning, with the autumn sun making a welcome appearance. I decide not to waste the weather and get myself ready for a walk to the park. It's getting on for ten before I'm out of the door. The bright sunshine does nothing for the bite in the air, but I soon warm to a steady walk. There's the usual splattering of people, mostly heading in Aldi's direction. The park is surprisingly deserted considering the weather. A couple of ladies come into view, chatting as they briskly walk away from me. I try not to dawdle, brisk walking saves my free time and gives me some sort of exercise. As I'm going round I give mam a call, she comments on my heavy breathing with a "Silly bugger" that makes us both laugh. It takes about twenty minutes to walk around the park, and I'm soon back home into the warmth of the flat. I make myself a couple of rounds of toast, and a tea then catch up with my sister Denise. We're both on our own, and although I think we manage the loneliness quite-well, it's always nice to chat. We both have the same sense of humour, and generally we both have a moan at anything and everything. It's soon lunchtime , I'm not hungry so I just make a coffee and put on the television. I'm looking at my iPad as I press the on button of the controls, so it's a few seconds before I realize the tv hasn't come on. I grab the remote to again press on, and there, for a slit second, I see the green and red men. The pictures are back to normal now, but I dare not take my gaze from the screen, expecting something to happen. I keep watching for a while, but there's nothing. As the afternoon wears on, I find myself getting rather tired, I think about picking my guitar up, but am really not in the mood, and before long I've dropped off.

I wake mid afternoon to a silent flat. The tv had switched itself off as it does after a while. The bright day has given way to a dim dreary day, I turn to look at the window behind me, it's pitch black outside. I turn to look at the clock, just past quarter to three.

I pick up my mobile, thinking a new battery is needed for the clock. But no, two forty seven. I walk over to the window, all I see is blackness, not a night time blackness, but it's as if the window had been painted black. I move into the bedroom and over to the window, then hastily to the kitchen. Total darkness. I take a few deep breaths to calm myself before I move over to the door, and open it.

I stand there frozen, for what seems like ages as I'm confronted by V. How I know I can't say, but I know. The image is not clear, and anyone else seeing it without the knowledge of V, would think it was me, but I know it isn't. The image, as with the mirror, mimics my movements, it's as if I'm looking through frosted glass. I wonder if I should say something? If V needs me to start whatever is next, but there's something about V's eyes. They're not shut, but looking down, then!!!. He slowly looks up and into my eyes, "You know now that I am real, I will show you so you will have no doubt". With that the image begins to move forward away from the darkness. I slowly step back to allow him into the flat. The blur of the image has now gone, and I see V has my form. What V's real form runs through my mind. "I have been sent here to stop you, you can not sustain the way you treat life, life will fight back, you are losing the fight". "Losing the fight for what?" I yell. There is an uneasy pause before, " I can not process a response without guidance from Life". I begin to understand the confusion V has experienced. I stay quiet waiting for more information, " if you lose the fight , life will be affected. With that, the room begins to lighten. I turn to the window to see the brightness returning. I turn back, and V has gone.

V says that I should have no doubt, am I convinced?, that it's not just in my head, as I think it, I have the need to open the door, why?, I haven't a clue. I open it to see the lobby where V had stood. Everything's normal, but as I close the door my eyes are turned to the floor, and a set of footprints, one green, one red. Daring not to take my eyes off the footprints and wishing I had my phone with me I manoeuvre myself-into a position to keep the prints in view while I slowly walk backwards to my phone. After fumbling for a few seconds I have it in my hand. I bring up the camera without taking my eyes away from the doorway. I walk over to the door, point the phone , expecting the prints to disappear at any moment, I press!!! As if V is toying with me, at that point the prints do disappear. I'm crushed and fall to my knees in hopelessness. Then I look at the phone, and there, in the bottom corner is a little square where the last photo is displayed. Do I dare press it? Anger begins to well up inside me. I touch the square, and there is the image of the footprints, exactly as I saw them. I spend the next five minutes going from one thing to another on my phone, then going back to the photo, checking that it's still there, I even switch it off and back on again. It's still there. Is this my proof?

CHAPTER 11.

At last I have some answers. The messages from V were more coherent. He talks of 'Life', and also the fact that he is a messenger with someone or something his controller. I begin to get the feeling that I am not the problem, or not wholly anyway. Maybe just a part of V's problem, life's problem.

I wish I could get help from someone else, but who would believe this. Even if I show them the photo they would still think I was off my head. I know if someone bought this to me, I would definitely think they were mad. I focus my thoughts on 'Life', trying to come up with some sort of answer to what it could be. If I take thing literally, then we are talking of something threatening our lives, threatening death. This is the first time that I can see a link with the virus. Are we responsible for the virus ourselves? bringing the thoughts of many that it's man made. I find it difficult to understand, after four years of the virus, V has waited so long. V exists, not in a human, physical way. If he was, we would surely know. So, in a spiritual way, some sort of entity, that lives, but needs to mimic a physical appearance.

I have much going on in my head. I need to take a break. So I put on the kettle and make a coffee. The light now has gone, and I draw the curtains, the limited but normal view gives me a good feeling. I switch on the lights and settle on the sofa. I put on the tv and check the news on my iPad, After, I had checked that the photo was still there. The government continue to stress that news is independently reported. We all know that is complete rubbish, and you must be either part of the government, rich, or completely daft. The world economy has been decimated, but of course there's still the Haves and Have Nots. When the virus first struck, it was clear that the elderly and chronically ill people were most at risk. The inability for governments to act quickly, especially in care homes, caused so many fatalities, as the virus ripped through the homes. Different-races were affected differently, with the Indian population hit badly, mainly due to to the closeness of families. Indeed, those countries that had the most diverse populations were hit the worst. Governments announce death rate numbers far fewer than the actual death toll. We are told by Boris that the worlds death toll is over seven million, when the real total is ten times that of seventy million. Government are no more than dictatorships, rebellions are quickly dealt with. More prisons than hospitals built since it started, tells its own story. It's a mess. Could this be why V is here?.

The evening moves on at pace, after a late dinner I get myself settled to bed. The usual array of nibbles set out on the bedside table. I'm feeling quite relaxed, worry about earlier events not causing me too many problems. I'm hoping V has moved away from that dream, now we have made our first meeting. Maybe I can get another stress free night. I check the

tv channels and settle down to Lewis, and
in no time at all, I'm asleep.

CHAPTER 12.

I wake at eight thirty, and apart from the usual excursions to the bathroom, it's been a peaceful night. As I get a coffee and move into the lounge, taking time to look at my Mary. My walls are draped with photos and paintings. It's been ten years since I lost her, time hasn't lessened the pain. She never deserved the terrible time she had, what she went through stays with me. I remember praying, but nobody heard. As I said, I have photos of me and Mary, on some of our lovely holidays, including one with her and my sister Denise, we were on holiday with my mam. It was taken the day before she became ill. It still doesn't seem real.

Looking round at the walls in my lounge where I have a few of my oil paintings hanging. On the sideboard, a few of my pottery efforts including a life sized bust of my head that has an eerie look to it. The lounge is small with a large cupboard, a tv stand and a small table. My acoustic and Fender guitars stand in corners, my eight track recorder under the table. I don't keep the flat tidy, Mary would be horrified. The kitchen and bathroom are adequate. The bedroom has a large wardrobe and a double bed. The space in the flat is minimal but doesn't excuse the mess. I've been here in Talby, a small village on the outskirts of the city since 1998. Although small, it has everything I need. The daily bulletin tells of new no go areas, suggesting a new local outbreak, but nothing that affects me. It's shopping day today, so thoughts turn to my requirements. My diet is anything but healthy, as ease of preparation overrides a healthy lifestyle. I roughly set out a list for mam, as I did for myself. Seldom do the lists change to any degree. I've an early spot this week, eleven till twelve. Thinking of my week and all that is gone, reminds me that I've hardly used my car, and that the petrol saved means I can have a nice run out to look forward to.

V is fast becoming a part of life. I find it difficult to fear, which is so not like me. I've always turned and run from conflict, at time been nothing more than pathetic. Maybe I'm still denying that this is all real, despite everything. But all the unbelievable things he's done should make me fearful I know. I pick up my phone and go to photos, I'm half hoping it's gone and all this isn't real. But no, it's there. At this point I'm distracted by the background sound of the tv, when I hear that name, Trump. As unbelievable as the virus, this maniac has become as infamous as Genghis Khan, Stalin, and Adolf Hitler. The beating of the virus days after he had tested positive, propelled his belief that he was some kind of chosen one, the new messiah, the one who would save humanity. What better a country to succeed in his madness, America. They believed him, followed him, voted for him. He closed all access to the states. Built walls to keep others out and fought the virus, seemingly for the Americans, and they ran head long into his madness. Black lives matter soon became, Black lives matter so they can serve the white Americans. But the whites soon saw how far he would go to put down any uprising, they finally realize they were following a maniac. His dictatorship didn't keep the virus out, but held it in, killing millions of all races. When they finally got him out of the White House, they found stone masons carving a statue, his statue, to replace Abraham Lincoln's.

As ever, my mind is full to overflowing. I have to admit to being a bit of a daydreamer, finding it a lot easier than the real thing. I suppose you'll be thinking I'm about to move towards my mental state, and V is just another escape from reality. Oh I would love to say you're right, but I'm afraid I can't hide from this, and I have to face it, there's no escape. I spend a lot of time thinking why me, surely I'm the most unremarkable person to help V to resolve in some way his life threatening situation. 'Life', now that's an interesting way he describes V's boss, but of course, we now know that he's just a messenger. Shit!!!, I suddenly remember the shopping, and I hastily sort myself and set off.

Today I will be taking mams shopping straight to her. We, as a family, have set out a quite rigid structure of contact, to minimize the risk, not only to my mother, but as Amanda and Paul, my kids say, "You and Denise aren't spring chickens," and of course, at seventy and seventy three, they're right. But there's no doubt that having a very tight structure, is far easier for mam to understand. I'm soon moving round the store and I'm at the check out in no time at all. After a stop at the petrol station, I set off to mams. Talby is some six miles from her flat, where she lives on the outskirts of the city. The rest of the family are all within a few minutes of her. I unlock the door and am greeted with a "Hi ya", I put the shopping onto the kitchen worktop. My mam still does for herself, making her own dinners. My sister does her cleaning now, but for a ninety nine year old, she's incredible. I sit and chat about the usual things, and she asks after the kids, who I'm glad to say keep in touch by phone, on a regular basis. Occasionally they will come to her flat and stand at the bottom of her stairs, she particularly likes that. I stay for an half hour or so before making my way to the car. Having not used much petrol last week, I decide to have a drive out. I go a usual route towards Butterworth, then join the M1 back to Talby.

As I merge onto the M1, Suddenly there's an almighty CRACK!!!. My car takes off, spinning out of control. I hit a barrier side on, rolling the car over and over till I eventually lose consciousness.

CHAPTER 13.

When I come round I'm sitting on the grass verge with a blanket round me. All I can see is devastating carnage everywhere. A large lorry was on its side, with what looks like a Volkswagen, with its roof compressed into its seats. There's cars all over the carriage way, with tangled pieces of metal everywhere. There are screams coming from one of the cars as firemen attempt to free the trapped people. I look in horror at three blankets covering what could only be fatalities. I stand up and walk towards the carnage. There's blood everywhere. Firemen dowsing the lorry with foam, suggesting chemicals of some sort might ignite, and to my total disbelief, there, almost unrecognizable, is my Saab. I just stand there in shock. It looks like it's been through one of those crushers. "Sir!" booms out, "You need to get back to the verge". It's a police women. She turns me round and walks me to a place away from the site. She tells me to stay there and that they will be with me shortly. I unwrap myself from the blanket and check my body for injuries, there's none, not a scratch. How can this be? My car is crushed to half its size. Maybe I was thrown out before the impact. But I'd still have some sort of injury, but I've not.

There's no way, its not humanly possible for me to survive this, and then I realize. V has saved me, it's the only answer.

An ambulance lady walks toward me, "Are you ok sir?" "That's my car", pointing to what's left of it. I answer, "How can I be?". "You've been very lucky". There's not a scratch on me. I again ask how can it be, but she has no answer. I thank her as she moves away. I notice a police man stop her, asking her questions, probably about me, and once they're finished talking he moves towards me. "We need to get you off the carriage way sir, although you seem not injured. They want you to be checked out at the hospital." He leads me to the back of an ambulance where another man is loaded into the back, he's talking, and doesn't seem too badly injured. I step in and sit opposite, "You ok", I say, immediately wishing I hadn't. "That bloody lorry pulled out straight in front of me, no bloody indicators". He didn't say another word all the way to the hospital.

They lead us to an area that is clearly designated to the pile up. I see several people lying on beds surrounded by doctors and nurses. I take a seat. There's a lot of badly hurt people, I could hear their pain. I feel strange being there with no injuries, at which point a, police officer walks up to me. He asks for my name, address and registration number, he taps away at his tablet, gone are the days of the pencil and pad. It was clear that he hadn't been at the scene, so no point in asking questions. With that he moves away to another one of the people being treated. "You want a drink lovey?", comes from an elderly lady pushing a trolley, I nod my head and smile, she pours me a drink and I thank her. Another rush of voices sees a further casualty, a woman, who looks in a bad way. I notice the lady that had talked to me at the scene, catching her eye I gesture her over to me. "What happened ?" I ask. I can't remember anything of the crash and what caused it, hoping that I wasn't to blame. She told me that it seems like the driver of the lorry fell asleep, hit a barrier sending him across the carriageway, before he turned over. Then several cars hit him at high speed, "You were very lucky, very lucky indeed". Saying what I already knew, there were fatalities. After a long wait I was eventually seen by a nurse who took my blood pressure and so on. Shortly afterwards I was allowed to leave.

So what now? I run through my options to get home. I'm not keen on a taxi, being in an enclosed space with a stranger. I can't call anyone, no way I want to explain what's happening, well, not at this time anyway. Just then a car draws up next to me. "Stephen, I am to take you home, V is waiting". There's an inevitability to any argument I could put for not getting in the car. I duck my head as I enter the car, turn, and sit, but I'm not on the car seat, no, I'm on my sofa, at home. Not only am I at home but there's a newspaper on my knee. I pick it up to read the lead headline, 'Six die in horror crash'. It is clearly my accident, photos say so. Then, slowly, the flat begins to shake to V's voice. "PROOF, YOUR PROOF".

I'm stunned into silence before I scream at the top of my voice. "You Bastard!!!. You didn't have to kill all those people. What do you want from me, I can't do this, I can't help you. I'm weak, pathetic , why in God's name me?". I'm drawn towards my bedroom and sit on the bed in front of a large mirror. I half expect to be face to face with V, I'm not mistaken. The image once more mimics me, but the eyes give it away, they're worried, finding everything difficult. This from a being who is capable of doing all these things. Then V speaks "We did not cause the accident. We used the situation so that you will know we exist. The people would have died even if we didn't use it.". I think a while then nod my head as I begin to realize that maybe the crash wasn't caused by V. " I have been put here by Life, to stop your kind from doing Life harm. "You are heading towards oblivion, but are not able to stop it. We can not allow this to happen. The thing you call virus warns you. Your kind fails to work together, even when you're faced with oblivion. I am put here to allow you to change, to help save yourself from your stupidity. You are part of Life. He will continue without you, but it will hurt Life. You cannot survive without Life. My function is to teach, so you will see how to change. I will guide you, and soon be able to show you what has to be done, so that you can survive".

The virus warns us? I wonder if this could all be to do with our systematic rape of our planet, and climate change that the virus is not the main concern of V, but our treatment of our planet is. My mind lightens the mood to think of Mary's view on climate change, and those 'tree huggers' as she wryly called them. If our abuse of the planet is causing distress to something or someone not of our world, I can see that would be a problem. Maybe this is that first contact. I want to laugh at that but out of this world things are exactly what has happened since those first dreams that started all this. So, am I now looking at visitors from another planet? They would be far in advance of us. Why would they need, or want to protect our world, and the fact that if they don't, it somehow will have an adverse affect on them (V/Life).

I suddenly realize where I am. I look at the mirror and my reflection tells me V has gone. I move into the lounge and over to the window. My Car!!! it's there, parked, undamaged. Of course it is. The day seems to have been full of V, but the reality is it's only in my head. The contact, although intense, covers only a few moments in time. My eyes move to the paper in my hand as I read on about the crash and the view of one driver who had witnessed the crash, and how she saw a man who seemingly was, unbelievably unharmed. It seems certain that I was there, and that it was V's attempt to convince me he's real, and not just in my head. It was also another reason for me to believe he meant me no harm. Yes I know he had put me through such fear, but V is learning, feeling his way. It seems he has, like me, learnt a great deal since it started. V's use and understanding of words has truly grown. I begin to browse my growing list of our contact, looking at it, hopefully in a more positive way. That sound stupid I know, I'm far from understanding what all this is about. I drift into a little normality as I put the kettle on. I check my phone, not only for the time but the date as well. Not that V is totally to blame for that, most people lose what day it is these days. I grab my drink and settle on the sofa. My mind brings up the dream that first started it all, and begin to see some of its meaning. The magic carpet flight around the earth. The red and green people though, I've still no idea. V is a messenger for Life. I'm desperately trying to link up things but it does look like he is very close to getting across why he is here, and what it's all about. However, he has made it clear that we are heading for Oblivion.

v

CHAPTER 14.

I decide that a walk to clear my head is required. There's about enough daylight left of the day. It'll be cold, so plenty of layers are needed. My walk, as usual, takes me to the local park. There are other walks that take you into the countryside, but I'm a creature of habit, and never get fed up of Bouskell park. Before the virus it was mainly used by dog walkers, but since the outcry concerning the virus and pets, dogs are a rare sight. The winter sun has very little heat, but the brightness eases the soul. I stop to watch a couple of squirrels chasing each other between trees and hedgerow, without being chased by dogs. The trees, almost bereft of leaves now give winter its feeling. What leaves are left fight against the breeze, as they hold on to autumn. It's difficult not to think about what's happening, and even stranger that I've been chosen. As I told V, I have to be the most incompetent person to get things done, and the thought of me having to save the world, well, stupid. I can only think that V hadn't the power to pick who he contacted. Suddenly I'm hit by a wave of fear, loss and helplessness, one thing I haven't missed since V contacted me. It's a cross I have carried since my early teens. Living with depression left me with a fear that still haunts me to this day. Medication helps, but at a cost, subduing the fear, but also the real me. Sorry, I'm sure you don't want to listen to this rubbish.

It takes about an hour for a couple of circuits of the park and then to get home. I feel refreshed and ready for food. I'm not a structured eater, mainly eat when I'm hungry, and I'm hungry. I can't be bothered with anything too complicated, so I rustle up my favourite, beans on toast. Sad or what?. I settle on the sofa as the news begins. The tv is pretty much on constantly while I'm in the flat. Silence isn't a friend of mine, using the noise to block out the fear that runs through my life. There's more harrowing news of new outbreaks in Africa. The lack of health care in vast areas of the country, leading to the worst death toll. V's talk of us "not working together" booms out in my head, as the rich hold on to their wealth and lives, while the rest perish.

There's a deep fear that runs through me, but my calmness suggests V is looking after me, or should I say 'Life' is looking after me. As the day draws into night, it seems to have gone on forever. I'm hoping that there's no more to come from V, or now, 'Life'. I wonder if contact with life will be different, as far as I know, he's the main man. I finish my food and after taking my plate to the kitchen, I settle on the sofa to watch tv. As usual I'm shattered, and soon find myself beginning to drop off. Am I awake, or am I dreaming?.

My thoughts on 'Life" are soon answered as!!!, "You are unable to see me, but I am here. You are safe, I will keep you so". Whether or not I'm awake or dreaming I try to open my eyes, but it's clear I'll only see something when 'Life' is ready. I feel my heart pounding, I link it to the beat of the light from the dream. Although not being able to see, I feel I'm being lifted, pulled upwards. It's like that awful part of a roller coaster when you're winched up to the top. It's quite eerily quiet. I still feel the sensation of being pulled up. I don't know just how long I'm being pulled up, but it feels ages. The silence more than anything is stressing me out. At that moment "You are safe, no harm will come to you", booms out. Clearly he knows my stress, probably he knows my every thought, which is rather unsettling in itself. Eventually I feel myself come to an halt. I wait. "Open your eyes, you are safe".

When I open them, there, in front of me, is an incredible sight. The most beautiful, spectacular colourful display I've ever seen. It's like I'm sitting on top of the universe, looking down on it's beauty.

"What you see is me, all you see enables me to be. They are my heart, my veins and all that I need to survive. This is me, but your actions impact on my well-being. Soon I shall show you what to do, so that your world will recover. Then your world and my world will become a more beautiful place. Now I will take you on a journey of wonder, so you will know what you are part of." I begin to move.

To describe what I am experiencing, no words can do it justice. I'm on a journey around the Universe. The colours drench what we know of space, black and white. It's anything but that. From a slow stroll my speed increases, faster and faster I travel until stars blur into green and red lines, my dream. I begin to slow to more incredible sights. I begin to make out a planet, our planet, Earth. As I dive ever closer, outlines of land and sea become clear. " I will now show you what could happen". As in my dream I begin to circle the earth. I'm travelling vast distances, continent to continent. As I pass where I started from, the view begins to change. Oceans growing, land reducing. The clear lines become hazy. A kind of mist descends around Earth, and with each pass, Earth is changed. "This need not happen. Your leaders do not work together, this can not continue. Your planet will not allow you to destroy it. It will rid itself of the cause. You!!!. Unless you change, it will not stop until the cause has gone. You cannot stop it with your drugs. Only through change can you stop the virus. If you change, I will stop the virus, and give you back your planet. Soon I will show you, and many others around your world, what you need to do."

V

I sense that 'Life' has said his final words for now. I am still sent on my way through the Universe, to the wonders that it holds. I soon begin to witness a pulsating light growing ever stronger, and all the beauty that it holds. I know I am passing the heart of 'Life'. As I pass and move away from the pulse, I begin to tire, eventually closing my eyes into sleep. I know that when I wake, I will be back in my home, to wait for V.

The reality of what 'Life' is, confronts my beliefs. Where does he originate?. Is this our maker, our God?. V is here to make us realize, and he's right, deep down inside we know the damage we are doing to our planet. What has taken millions of years, has been destroyed in no more than a blink of an eye. It's been known for a while that something had to be done to stop the erosion of our planet by humanity.

The complexity of V is no more than a drug. An untried drug at that. Just as drugs we used to beat the virus had to evolve as we learned more about it. But of course, the virus is not the sole problem, our rape of the earth was as well. I have often thought about the Universe. The never ending Universe. How can something be never ending? It's too crazy to comprehend. Even though I know what 'Life' has shown me, where life ends and another begins, is still a mystery.

'Life' has made it quite clear that our planet has become a threat to its safety. We have become it's Cancer. It seems we are being given a chance by 'Life', although I'm not sure why. He feels that our planet, or more to the point, man, is worth saving. 'Life' has given me a lot of answers, he has told me that I am not alone, that there are many of us throughout the world. I'm comforted that I'm not alone, and everything V will ask of me, will be shared throughout our world.

When I wake, I am as expected, back home. It's incredible, the whole thing is overwhelming, but I know I must be ready to follow V. I've completely forgotten what day it is and have to check my phone. I click on the kettle, grab a mug, and pour a coffee. Wondering what today will bring, I head to the window. The morning looks bright, the sun shining on frosty trees makes a beautiful picture. I think that all this could be over for humanity. How we're going to save this runs through my head, but I must stay focused and wait for V. I can't deny that a part of me is excited. Excited!!!? How can I be? What I have gone through, the fear imbedded in me by

V. Then he shows me I am in no danger. I can go round in circles with all this.

Waiting is almost unbearable. I feel on edge. I suppose if I didn't, I would be weird. There's no way it seems that I can keep my thoughts from V, and all that's gone on away from him. I occasionally think that I must be special in some way, for V to have chosen me. I know that's not true. Who in their right mind would put the world's future in my hands. I wonder how the others who have been chosen are coping. I imagine they're just as amazed and confused as I am. I get a funny glow as I remember that incredible sight, as I was shown who, and what 'Life' is. I wonder how V will show himself next. Will he come like before, or. Stop that!!!. I try to pull my thoughts back, trying to tell myself that I will know soon enough, what's to be done.

Minutes and hours drift by, mingling into each other, with the anticipation ruling my thoughts. I take note of a news update, seeing that infection rates rise again. As we head towards winter, I wonder what exactly V will do to stop the virus, and this wholesale cull of humanity. Surely he must address this horror, I can't see how we could turn things round while still fighting the virus.

The evening draws in at a pace as I draw the curtains, and switch on some lighting. There's the usual stuff on the box, old detective series, black and white movies of years back. Occasionally I watch some comedy, but laughing hasn't been upmost in my life since Mary died. But right now my thoughts are elsewhere. Is this the night, does it start here, now. Will we get another chance or is it far too late for humanity to survive?.

I tire as I wait for my next instructions. But before that, I need to tell you the real story of the horror of this virus. It needs to be told. It's easy to get lost in government's rules, lies, hatred and blame. The terrible cost of lives, each and everyone lost brings destruction to families, to loved ones. Each a tragedy in itself, touching so many lives. After the initial wave, there was a relaxing of all things that had kept the virus in check. We became complacent, let our guard down. We relied too much on a vaccine, a vaccine that had to be continuously tweaked as it mutated. But we now know the truth that no matter how we changed the vaccine, the virus would win. Our planet was fighting back. Ridding itself of humanity's rape of it. I wonder, fearfully, how 'Life' will stop our destruction. But I somehow know that he can, and that this is 'Life's' gift to us, if, we change how we treat our world.

It was true about becoming complacent. I believe the vast amount of us we're guilty, including me. From derelict streets to busy shopping centers, schools and pubs opened, far too early by far. It was easy to blame, but those in charge were in a no win situation at that point. But the government was slow to react at the beginning. Eventually, after many lives lost that seemingly could have been saved, they began to take control more and more. First with the virus, and then when it became clear that rather than beat it, we had to live alongside it. Gradually restrictions were imposed, initially asking us to follow guide lines, but of course when the virus started to spread uncontrollably governments started to blame the people, and seized their chance to take control. First they imposed fines, but these soon changed, squeezing us into whatever situation they wanted. They began to use the army to police the situation. It was in the second year of the virus when live ammunition was distributed to the armed forces, and the first legal murder was perpetrated. Shops were closed, Sainsburys, Morrison's, Asda, all closed. Aldi became the only store left. At first people were fine with it, Aldi was by far the cheapest store, but as prices rose, questions were asked, eventually uncovering why that just one store was used. The complete government cabinet had become share holders in Aldi. The governments of course denied it, but restrictions were imposed to stop cabinet members financial wealth being examined.

They now have complete power. Any opposition was quashed by the army, and rather than a building plan for new hospitals, the only buildings planned were prisons. I now wonder exactly how V will deal with this.

So this is where we are. Before V, well, no hope really. Knowing what we know now, there was no stopping the virus. It came to render the human race extinct. But it seems we are to be given a chance to save ourselves. And I wait for instructions.

Wait for 'LIFE'.

CHAPTER 15.

And so it starts!!!

The night passes without incident. But there's something. Something telling me it's begun. Since my first contact with V, I seem to have a kind of second sight about when things are about to happen. I lie for a while before dragging myself from my bed, and into the kitchen. As I wait on the kettle boiling I hear a noise coming from the lounge. Expecting something to happen I go to look. It's the tv. It's switched itself on. I sit and watch. There's a still picture on.

I've seen it before, on my journey through 'Life'. This is it. My mouth dries, drier than the desert. I quickly pour a drink. I pick the controls up, checking that the sounds up. I might have guessed, nothing works. V is now in charge.

The screen changes to a map of the world. Then!. "I talk to you all around your planet. I will tell you how to stop the destruction of your world but I will not cure your problem, that will be up to your kind. First you must have a blood test. I will make this possible, you will not be refused. I will enable your blood to target your virus. Nobody will know or think you are special. This is all you need to do for now, I will contact you you again." I ignore the beep on my phone, and sit there for a while before realizing there's not going to be anymore from V. For the first time for a while I feel alone, knowing that V won't be around for, I guess, some time. My thoughts turn to ringing the doctor to book a blood test. I hate having to deal with people, and my mind begins to practise what I'm going to say. Just then I remember the beep of a new text on my phone that came in while V was talking. Once again V is true to is word as the text reads "Reminder, you have an appointment with the nurse on Thursday the nineteenth of November at one forty five". I'm relieved and thankful. Once again I think just how many of us there are throughout the world. I guess that we will be given some kind of immunity to the virus, and that will be used in beating it. V made it clear that we're not the saviours of the human race, suggesting there are many more who have been visited by V. So it looks like, for a while anyway, I must go back to normality, until the virus is beaten. That of course isn't going to be easy. The fear that V has shown me, albeit unintentionally, doesn't dampen my excitement of what's to come.

I move to the kitchen for yet another coffee. The snap of the letterbox informs me I have mail. More junk, the virus hasn't diminished those trying to sell us stuff. My eyes are drawn to a coloured envelope. I kick it (post usually sits there for a couple of days before I touch it). It looks like another advert, but it's flap side down so there's no telling who it's from. I can't be bothered with the rigmarole of putting on gloves and spraying it. It's going nowhere anyway. It's Tuesday, Tuesday morning. Now that makes me think, is it just a coincidence?. Should I open it now? Tuesday's have always been a special time for me, ever since Kossoffs song, Tuesday Morning. It wouldn't surprise me if it wasn't just a coincidence, and V is using this morning because he knows it is special to me.

I'll have to look at it or it'll be bugging me all day. It's the bright colours drawing me too it, mainly green and red, of course. On go the gloves and out comes the anti bacterial spray. I pick it up and spray it liberally. The bulkiness also fascinates-me. I slide the letter opener across, and peer into the envelope, and pull out the contents. It's face masks. I didn't order any face masks. I open the sealed unit and pull one out. They're pretty standard masks, yet they have a strange colouring, the likes I'd not seen before. There are just the two of them, they're the kind you can wash. There's nothing else. Nothing to say where they're from. Strange, very strange.

I look around the flat, it's a mess, as usual. I decide on a tidy up, more to occupy my mind than anything else. I tend to have a day to blitz the place every now and again, I'm not good at tidying as I go. I collect pots from various rooms and begin to wash up. I clear the rubbish and put on the washing machine and finish with the vacuum. I've begun to be a bit of a slob. Well, that's not completely right, I am a slob. My Mary would be playing hell, but it's not easy for me. I've become lazy. Laziness has become a way of life for so many. It takes me about an hour to get the flat looking ok, ish.

It's soon early afternoon, so I get myself a drink and something to eat. I text my children and sister, before ringing mam. She's fine. She too has had a life dogged by depression. However since the virus she has managed her life well, and still enjoys life. I decide on a walk around the park. Sound boring I know, but I never get fed up with the place. There's always something new to see. There's not many people out. We are all given four hours each week for exercising. Passing another person has become rather stressful, and crossing over the road to the other side the norm. I'm stopped in my tracks when a women turns from a side street. The mask, that mask. I know what she's thinking, but for a moment we're too shocked to do or say anything. She moves towards me. "V?" she says. I nod my head. "I thought I was going mad". "No you're not going mad", I say, and also know that I'm not-mad either.

"It's so incredible and unbelievable", she says. I ask why she calls it V. It's just a name I gave it". "Me too", I tell her. "Maybe it's just a coincidence", she says. I reply, "V doesn't do coincidences". She smiles. "Do you think we are meant to meet", she asks. I tell her "Yes, the masks, it's what they're for. We need to talk". I take out my wallet and one of my old business cards. I ask her "Shall I put it on this wall?" "No " she says and walks up to me and takes it from my hand. "I'm Steve", "Diane, Di". She turns and walks away, turns her head, "I'll call". She turns the corner.

I've completely gone off a walk, so return home. I'm not sure what I'm thinking at the moment. I had started to think that I could start to relax now, for a while anyway, while V sorts the virus. Now I have to talk to someone new. I'm not good with new people. I can feel the stress creeping up already. I don't know why I said we had to talk. I'm going to be on edge I know, wondering if and when she'll call. Why does V want us to know each other, he surely does, I know he's orchestrated it. I try to clear my head, and yes, you guessed it, another coffee. For a moment the thought of a large vodka enters my head and I think maybe I would if I had some in, but thankfully I've not. Drink has been a problem before. I'm tired and worn out.

After a quiet half an hour trying to calm myself, things seem easier, and I decide that meeting Diane may be good. I've found it impossible to talk to anyone about it. It's something I'm sure, we both need. V knows that. Sweet child of mine

rings from my phone, "Hi, Steve, it's Di."
I say "Hello". "I'm glad I have someone
to talk to at last, I've been struggling with
it all, thinking I was going mad". I tell
her that V has seen us struggling, and is
looking after us. I ask how long had she
known. "The twentieth of October. I had
this dream. Are you afraid?". "Oh yes,
who wouldn't be", I tell her. I go on to tell
her how V had put me through hell at the
beginning, but that I now know he was
learning. "How is he doing all this? what's
going to happen?" I tell her that nothing
will happen to her, and that I believe in V
who is here to help us, not to destroy us.
"If he wasn't he wouldn't be here now".
There's a silence. "Sorry, I must sound
like some pathetic hysterical woman." I
assure her that it's not the case. "Do you
have my number?" "It's on my phone".
I read it to her. "Can I call again?". I let

her know that she can call at any time, and that I'm just as glad I have someone to talk to about everything.

I feel relieved as I hang up. It wasn't as stressful as I thought, and now I can at last have someone to talk too. It does seem that Diane is actually worse than I am, which doesn't worry me, I'm a good listener and helping her will be good for me. Although masked, I would say Diane is a lady of some age, not as old as me perhaps, late fifties, early sixties. She has a slight form, suggesting that she looks after herself. Although sounding nervous, she's softly spoken. I remember to save her number into my phone and also in my iPad. Memories not as good these days. I rummage round seeing what's to eat. I decide on a curry ready meal. I eat far too much rubbish, but it's difficult to motivate myself since I've been on my own. I, as usual, take my food to eat in bed while watching tv. Afterward I begin to feel tired, and concentrating is difficult. I settle down, and sleep takes over.

CHAPTER 16.

Wednesday seems to drag on for so long, with nothing really happening. What a difference a day make, I would have given anything for a quiet day before 'Life's' showing. Diane did call though, and we began to get to know each other. But other than that, it's been the most normal day since it all started. I'm not expecting any contact, and that does allow me an evening with the tv, before the day is done and I'm asleep.

Thursday. I see today as the beginning of reality. The day that becomes of substance. Not only in "Life's' world. But now with my blood in humanity's world. I wonder how long, how fast this first step will take. I can daydream a scenario, and I'm sure I will. I'm a dreamer, always have been. It's probably held me back from actually doing things. More than anything I think it's laziness, it's far easier to dream than to do. I'm not going to change now though. I'm guessing things to do with V are going to move a lot slower now that humans have been bought into the equation, after all, even if the first person who looks at my blood and shouts "THIS IS THE ANSWER". There's months of trials, government gagging news of a breakthrough, while they find a way to make them seem like they saved humanity, plus, how to make stacks of money. It's going to be interesting how V will set about dealing with them. I know these things will happen if V lets them, but I'm getting the feeling he won't.

I continually check the time on my phone, keen to get the test done and the process started. I wonder how all the others like me and Diane are handling it. I wonder when she'll ring again. V has got things moving, attacking the virus with our blood. My phone rings. It's Diane. "what time is your test?" I tell her, "Mine is two o'clock. Do you think they'll be others?". I wouldn't be surprised, but I tell her not to worry, that she doesn't have to talk if she doesn't want to, and that they will know and won't engage her. "You did". "We were both confused Di, and afraid. V knew that. He'll also know whether you want to talk or not. He won't let anything you don't want to do happen". "Do you feel any better now we have met?". I tell her that I was desperate to offload all the stuff that I'd been through, and my mind felt like it was going to explode. "I'm sorry you're having to go through this, but yes, I am glad we met". "I do feel better for talking. I did have an appointment with the doctor, but I couldn't bring myself to tell him all about this, I just told him that I was having bad dreams and felt depressed. It was a waste of time. I honestly thought I was going mad until I met you. I'm on my own, I have a son but he's not a very good listener". "I know what you mean. I have a close family, but they would think I was going mad if I tried to tell them, so I'm just as relieved to have met you. I'm on my own too, on Elm Street in a flat". "Do you have children?" "I've a son and daughter, grandchildren, a sister, and my mother is still going strong. They all live in the city". "How did it all start for you?". "It was just a dream" "You were flying, right?" "Yes, it's unbelievable I know, but we must accept it. If we try to work out how and why, we'll go mad. I think there will be a quiet period after the tests, maybe some time to come to terms with it" "I hope so". We chat for a little longer before we end our call.

I do myself some toast and a drink. It's half twelve, just over an hour till my test. I relax on the sofa, checking the news. Nothing much is happening any different than normal. I do think that maybe they'll be a quiet period until the blood thing brings any changes. I wouldn't be surprised if there was more contact from V. I probably shouldn't think too much on that subject but try to take this time to rest. Of course that won't be easy. I extract myself from the sofa and get ready to go to the doctors. I need to time it just right, I don't want to be early and have to wait, the virus still has fear for me, I'm of the age that it loves. I take the car so I can wait in it, although the surgery is only a couple of minutes away. I enter the surgery exactly on time. I'm passed by a middle aged man, he has a mask on, but not that mask. But as I relay my name to the receptionist, I see two more men, and they do, have that mask on. Both acknowledge that they have seen me. I nod my head, but not wanting to engage in any conversations, I move into the other, empty waiting room and sit down. I wonder what they will have make of me not going in with them, but those thoughts are quickly ended when a beep signals my turn. I knock and enter. "Mr Cewell, routine blood test". I had already removed my coat so she's straight down to the task. "That's it Mr Cewell, results in about a week". I wonder, results for what?, but don't ask. I say thank you and leave. I glance and again acknowledge the one remaining man in the waiting room as I leave. I'm soon home. I take off my coat and sanitize my hands, then spend the next hour or so in a bit of a daze really but very glad that the test is done.

I'm tired now, very tired, and all of a sudden I begin thinking negatively. I'm not sure where it's come from but the "Why Me!" shouts out loudly in my head. If I could walk away from this, I would. Maybe having time to think, isn't such a good idea. God, I could do with a drink, but of course that's a no no. I've been on the wagon for years, that would have bought a load of applause from those at CA, but I could well have been in trouble if I had some in. However, it's the memory of what you go through that keeps you off the stuff. My thoughts are interrupted by the sudden switching on of the tv, and that picture of the earth worms to V's sound. "All tests have been collected. The destruction of the virus will soon begin. You will ignore any reports that come from your leaders, as we begin to control their actions. All is well. You have now, all been joined together to work together, and give support and friendship. I will contact you again in seven days. 'Life' thanks you all." And at that, the tv switches off.

No sooner had the message ended than Diane calls. "What do you think he means?". "I trust V now. I would imagine to get the whole world to beat the virus, there has to be a coming together. America, Russia, China. It's not going to be straight forward. Try not to worry. They'll be loads of rubbish talked. I can see the Americans announcing they have saved the world. It's going to be that sort of thing. That's why V is telling us not to listen to it. I know it won't be easy, but just do what you're doing now, and call me. I'll do the same". "Ok, I'll try". "You seem to be handling it. I can't seem to stop thinking bad things are going to happen to us". I try to put her mind at rest, and we talk for several minutes more. We begin to talk of things other than V. Diane, like myself has lost her partner, being on her own for over five years. I tell her about losing Mary. It's nice to talk of other stuff. I feel we are really getting to know each other, something we're both happy with.

It's my shopping day. I call mam. She's fine. There's a few extras she needs this week. I text the rest of the family, and it's all good there too. After making our lists, I get a drink and switch on the tv. I suppose I'll be expecting news from now on. I pick up my guitar, and bang out a burst of Seagull. I fell in love in the seventies with a rock band, and rock music. It's a part of my life that stays strong to this day. I love the electric guitar, my only regret is my inability to play it to something like a good level. All Right Now, by rock band Free, and in particular guitarist Paul Kossoff, sold their music to me hook line and sinker. To this day, their music sounds as good now as back then. It's somewhere I can go when things get bad.

CHAPTER 17.

The next few days pass without incident, and as much as it can be, life had been normal. There's very little new news coming from the government, nothing anyway to suggest that the blood tests are changing things. I have however been getting to know Diane. We've talked most days and are getting on well, phone wise anyway. She seems really nice. I did however make the mistake of thinking that she had lost her husband, when in fact they had split. I didn't quiz her on why. She has three children, two girls. They live in other suburbs of the city. The girls are both married with one child each. The son is on his own. I get the feeling that there's not complete harmony between her family, and that the split may be the reason. She's really been hit badly with the solitude the virus has caused. And probably the last thing she would have needed was V. She says I'm handling it. She doesn't see what's inside. But I am probably handling it better. I have toyed with asking her to meet up on the park, but haven't plucked up the courage yet.

It's evening as I speak. I change channels onto the news. There's still no expected news, although the final article did catch my attention. It seems that there's going to be a meteor shower, which will give a spectacular sight in the sky tonight. I make a note of it and put a reminder on my phone. I'm just finished doing that when Di calls. "Did you see the news about the meteor shower tonight?". I reply in the affirmative, telling her it depends on the weather. "It's clear out at the moment, I've been out and looked. I would love to see it". There's an uneasy silence. "I thought I might go over to the park if I can pluck up the courage, but it's going to be dark over there". I tell her it's a good idea, and ask her if she wanted to meet up there. I hear Di giggle. I tell her not to worry, and that I didn't think I could go there on my own too. We arrange to meet at quarter to ten. After we had finished talking , the old nerves start to happen. I smile. You're seventy you idiot. Never the less there's time to wash my hair, clean teeth, and put on my best gear, which isn't that good to be honest. But it's going to be dark, thankfully.

V

I open up the window to check the temperature. It's cold. I put on my winter coat, not very fashionable, but warm. I leave a bit early so as not to be late. As I arrive at the park, there's a few people who I guess are there for the same reason. Luckily they're all pretty tall, making it easy to see that Diane isn't one of them. I'm only there for a few minutes when I see her walking towards the park. We greet each other, and I try to make small talk. I'm not good at conversations, especially if they're not family. I know what I want to say, but rarely does it come out that way. But Diane makes the running, and I begin to relax with her. I ask how she had been. Her answer boosts my confidence, talking about how she had felt so much better since we had met. We walk into the park carefully, glad of the moonlight. There's probably about a dozen of us out there, all heads turned to the sky. "There!!!", we turn to the figure pointing to the sky. Our eyes follow the pointing arm, and sure enough there's a glittering array of lights, similar to a firework. It makes the park substantially lighter. Our eyes follow the spectacle. Diane relays her glee at the spectacle, but as it intensifies, covering more of the sky, I sense a little uncertainty in her voice. "Is it alright?" I answer carefully, hoping to quell her doubts. But as I do the spectacle begins to slowly fade. As it does, the moon begins to be covered with clouds moving in, and the park becomes very dark. Suddenly, as we make our way to the entrance we are pitched into total darkness. All street lighting gone. No lights on any of the houses nearby. Di grabs my arm. For a moment, neither of us say a word. Then I tell her it's probably just a power cut. But I know differently.

V

Not only street and home lights are out, torches bought by some on the park are also out. Then there were two cars that seemingly had come to a dead stop. Di pulls at my arm. "Let's go, let's go home. She leads the way. Clearly we're going to Di's. Her walk become quicker as she hits familiar ground. She's-clearly frightened, as am I. "We're here". Already with her keys in her hand, she unlocks the door. Just then the light are back on. "There you go, a power cut, probably caused by the meteor-shower". She asks me if that could do that. "Yes, quite possibly", I reply. I stop at her door wondering if this is wise, Covid wise. But "Will you come in for a coffee?". I ask if she's sure. She says "Yes", and that it will be fine. "There's plenty of room, we can spread out". I nod, and she points to the lounge. "Make yourself at home. Tea or coffee?". "Coffee" I reply. I generally have coffee even when I'm out, it's to do with the milk. I have soya at home, so any kind of ordinary milk tastes funny to me. Di shouts that she only has normal coffee. "Thats fine thanks". There's a large sofa and a reclining arm chair in what is a good sized lounge. It's very tidy. It has the woman's touch. There's a large tv mounted on the wall. I notice photos standing on a sideboard, that I guess are her family. There's no table, but double glazed doors that I imagine lead into a dining room. She enters the room with her drink. "You can take your mask off". I get my first view of Diane unmasked. She's very easy on the eye. I remove my mask to drink. Di has sat on the sofa, well away from me, and I feel a little better about it. Neither of us comment on our unmasked state, apart from saying we don't like wearing them. "Shall I put the tv on?" I nod. She, as I do, searches for the news channel. As soon as she finds it comes news of a substantial power failure throughout the country. Major cities experiencing a twelve minute failure. Early reports suggesting the meteor storm responsible. "All power is now restored and the meteor storm has passed by", is the final say on it. "Do you think V is doing it?" I tell her that I don't know why, but yes I think V is responsible. Di asks if I had heard about Putin having Covid. I hadn't. We talk mostly about our contact with V. The similarities of our experiences are incredible.

We move from V and begin to talk about families. "Have you been on your own long". I had told her that I had lost Mary to illness. I was relieved that she didn't ask what was wrong with her. I hate talking about that awful illness. I tell her that she had been gone over ten years. I did ask about her marriage, and by the softening of her voice I get the feeling it wasn't what she wanted. I didn't delve any more on that subject, turning the conversation to children. I couldn't help noticing how relaxed and comfortable I was feeling. Usually I'm not good with new people. More and more I'm taking in the view. Di is lovely. I want to ask her age, but of course don't. My initial thought were probably a little high. I was hoping that the difference in age wasn't too much, (Listen to yourself, you muppet). Before we know it it's nearly midnight. "Time I was going", was followed by an uneasy departure, not knowing what to say or do. "I'll call you tomorrow if that's ok". "Yes please". She smiles. I walk home with a grin on my face, but remind myself not to get carried away again, remembering the pain and embarrassment of last time. It's well after midnight when I get home. First thing, medication. I need it to sleep. Taking it at this time will mean a late start in the morning. I'm soon in bed. Not sure what to make of tonight, but any thoughts are nice ones.

CHAPTER 18.

Saturday morning. I wake to the sound of the tv, and breaking news. It's not good. Putin, and that Chinese guy are dead!!!. That's not good. Diane had said about Putin having the virus. If V is responsible, that's not his best move. It's patchy as to how, and what happened, but by all accounts there had been rumours about both. No news was coming-from official sources within Russia as of yet. But scenes coming out of China, show masses of people seemingly mourning on the streets. My thoughts turn dark, and to the Cold

V

War. The virus first started in China, and Trump made scathing accusations, leaving no doubt that he held them responsible. There were also rumours that the virus was man made, by China. Tension between the three most powerful countries would be a worrying affair.

I need a bathroom break, and make myself a coffee. I move back to the lounge to continue watching. The news had moved on to the virus cases, increases in Britain above what would usually expected. It's the highest there's been for nearly two years and with death rates set to rocket in the coming weeks. Winter always increases the cases, but this is something else. A news conference is announced for five tonight, Boris's first for months. It looks certain that stronger restrictions will be announced, and even a new "Stay

Home" policy could come into force. The "Stay Home" state was implemented once before, a little over two years ago. Only medical reasons were allowed for anyone being outside. The "Delivery Army", was implemented, to deliver food and essentials. This was set up when the Stay Home rule was set up. It was a breeding ground for mental illness, with suicide rates soaring. At the time it was thought that the Stay Home policy would never be implemented again. Maybe I'm jumping the gun a bit, and should wait for the announcement at five. I run through the online news. There's growing numbers of reports throughout the world of mass deaths not being reported by the governments. Have we been deceived?. Has V been using us to clear humanity. I'm struggling to find any positive aspects of what V is doing. Increasing Covid deaths, causing unrest between governments. Di calls. "Let's wait to see what Boris says", I tell her. She's frightened, I'm frightened. I must admit that I can't see anything to suggest he's going to rid us of this plague. "Its only day three Di, V says he will contact us after seven, and he did tell us not to take any notice of the media". That's not putting either of us any more at ease, but what could I say. We talk for a while, and when she asks me round to watch the announcement at five I jump at the idea.

I arrive at Diane's about a quarter to five. I'm greeted with "Coffee, milk one sugar". I answer in the affirmative, I'm chuffed that she remembered. The tv is already on. " I can't believe it's got so bad so quickly". I reiterate my stance that I can't see why V would be causing this. It's a little after five before Boris appears. "I have to prepare us all for hard times. A report forwarded to me by the World Health Organization, confirms that covid 19 has mutated into a strain of the virus that is unaffected by any of the vaccines we have. The scientists are working tirelessly to find a new vaccine, and I have to say, making good progress. Unfortunately however, I must announce a further "Stay Home", lockdown of an unspecified length. I had hoped never again to order such a harsh practice. But I have no choice. No one must leave their homes, other than for medical reasons. Anyone with symptoms, must, contact the Covid Team. They will give you details what you need to do. The "Stay Home Army" have been activated, to bring food and essentials. I have to tell you that, anyone, found outside without a valid lawful reason, will be arrested and taken to secure Covid sites. I'm now going to hand over to our health minister Michael Strepson to run through what we know about this new strain of the virus". Diane and I turn to look at each other, and I'm afraid neither of us could be said to be giving the other one much confidence. But before we could say anything the screen changes. It's V. The picture of earth tells us so. "Life knows you are uncertain, afraid. You are in no danger. Now that the virus has mutated, he can begin the process of eliminating it. Do not listen to your governments, they do not know. In three days I will contact you again". With that V has gone.

We have no choice but to wait. For whatever reason V needs to know that we're ok. It seems that whenever there's doubt in our mind, he feels it. It's clear that he needs us. The question is why!.

"We won't be able to meet will we?", says Di. "I guess not. We have our phones". Anyhow I say, "Stay Home doesn't come in till midnight tomorrow, so they'll only be another day after that before we hear from V again. We'll know more then". I tell her not to worry. She smiles in a yeah I wish way. We continue to talk for ages. I find it easy talking to her. We get on to subject of relationships and marriages, suggesting that she couldn't do another one. I don't know whether she was just making it clear incase I had other ideas.

My walk home couldn't be more different than the night of the meteor storm. It seems I have, been getting ahead of myself where Diane is concerned. After a while of thinking, the thought of Diane being just a friend, take away any stress that I've been feeling. I had long decided that another relationship wasn't what I wanted. I suppose any thoughts I had of that, were more due to wanting something to distract me from V, Indeed, the more I think about it, the better I feel about it. After getting myself my evening meal, I settle down to some normal tv. One of the things Diane and I were talking about was not watching the news, and keeping away from the social media, so there's no news for me tonight. I'm not sure just how long I'll be able to keep that up though.

There's not an awful lot that I can relay to you over the next few days. There's been no more contact from V. The Stay Home enforcement took effect at midnight, on Sunday. It's already causing me problems trying to get through to order our shopping. I still have not got through. I used a visit to my mother as a excuse to get me out.

I had picked a medicine that she needs a few day ago. I am a volunteer for the NHS, not that I've done anything for them since the virus first struck. But I still have my lanyard, and wear it on most journeys. As it happened, I wasn't stopped. I've been talking to Diane a lot. Getting to know each other is a really good distraction for us both. It seems that she was born in Norwich, which is a nice coincidence. My aunt had spent most of her life there, and we were very close. I regularly visited her and got to know Norwich really well. Diane remembered a lot about when she was there, so we kind of knew what each other meant when talking about the area.

I'm not going to bore you with any more of this. So I skip forward to Tuesday night, and the thought of what tomorrow will bring. Day seven, and V.

CHAPTER 19.

Wednesday. Day seven. I wake early feeling awful, as always. Sleep was very fractured, impossible to get V from my mind. I switch on the kettle before moving to the bathroom. I'm hoping V won't be calling me before I'm fully awake. Di had wanted me to go round to her's for the day, but I managed to put her off, until the afternoon anyway, explaining that I'm not a morning person. I look around the flat. It's a tip again, pots piled high in the sink. Really need to tidy, but coffee first. I know I shouldn't be taking notice, but the number of new infections being reported is almost unbearable. It's not easy to ignore them. Over four years into this hell, and still governments can't work together. America and China at loggerheads, even without Trump in charge, especially with the recent death of China's leader. Maybe that not such a surprise, but European countries are not working together or sharing information. When a vaccine was first produced, there was some sort of togetherness. Countries like Britain, getting vaccine from all over Europe. But when the virus started to regularly mutate, new vaccines became hard to come by to the extent it's nigh on impossible to get it from another country. Countries are having to rely their own scientists. Of course, that puts the wealthiest countries first in line with each new vaccine, hence the imbalance in worldwide deaths.

There are differing reports of just exactly how many deaths the virus has caused worldwide. They range from forty to eighty million. There's no doubt in my mind that that the reality rests at the top of that range.

Suddenly I feel strange. I have to close my eyes as they begin to blur. I know this feeling, and I know I'm not alone. V is here. I don't need to open my eyes to see him, I can feel him.

"Stephen, open your eyes my friend. Do not be afraid". Strange as it might seem, I'm not. I slowly open my eyes. I gaze around at the most incredible view. Such wonder, colours so beautiful that it's impossible for me to relate to you just what I'm seeing. "The procedure has begun. I will tell you what has to happen. This is the only way 'Life' can prevent the loss of your species. He could not stop the infection as it was. He does not know how. He has added to it so it mutates into a virus he can defeat". It sounds like the truth. We know 'Life' has his limitations, so to change the virus to something he can beat makes sense. "I have told you that the virus is not the problem that you will need to address. You, are the problem. You must change.

'Life' has given you the means to defeat the virus. He can do no more. It will be up to your scientists and leaders to implement the new vaccine. It is the beginning of the changes that you have to make. You have to work together. I will show you how". V goes quiet, knowing I need time to think. So we now have the answer. But 'Life' cannot, or won't oversee its implementation. I fear that's not good. Regardless of the fact that we have got the answer, the super powers are still at each other's throats. How the hell is that going to change. I ask V how?, knowing us as he now does. "Your blood carries the antibodies to rid your world of this plague. Your people will come together. They will join together from each and every country. This will be what you, and those others we have chosen, will do. You are not alone, I am here to show you how to do this. I will contact you soon". I watch as the colours start to blur and slowly fade back to my flat.

I try to remember everything V has told me, knowing Diane will need to talk things through. Although it seems to make sense. I'm more thinking of how our powers to be are going to make this gift we have been given work. I'm struggling to realize why I'm not jumping for joy that the vaccine is here. I can't seem to think straight at the moment, and I'm feeling pretty awful. I head off to the kitchen to make a drink, but before I get there Di enters my head. I pick up the phone and call. She senses I'm worried, I apologize and let here know how I'm feeling. I'm hoping I don't make things worse for her. I needn't have worried, all of a sudden she becomes the rational one. She talks sense into me, showing a side of her I hadn't seen before, and before long we're having a bit of a giggle about it. "Ring any time", she says. I thank her.

Feeling a lot more relaxed, I get myself something to eat. I find myself rather bolting down my meal as my mind runs through multitudes of thoughts. I come up with yet another possibility, about what will happen. V says that his boss had to change the virus. He did that by using our blood. It can't be just coincidence that the massive rise in deaths should happen straight after our blood was taken. This thought is leading me to something I really don't want to face. Our blood, My blood, has altered the virus. The virus that now, has no working vaccine to combat it. My mind clears to a strange feeling of nothingness. I couldn't tell you just how long I sat there, but afterwards I had no knowledge of what thoughts had run through my mind. I was clearly in that state for a long period of time, because I am snapped out of it by the sound of the BBC news at ten. I've lost hours. Maybe those awful thoughts that I was in some way responsible for so many deaths, made my brain shut down, as a defence. I'm pretty confused at the moment. I really want this day to finish. I'm late taking my medication, but I'm not long to bed before I am at last asleep.

CHAPTER 20.

Before I know it, a new day is born. Rather than feeling rested, I feel pretty shell shocked. It's ten o'clock, I'm up later because of taking my medication late last night. I begin to think about the blood thing, but thankfully mam calls. "Hi mam, you ok?", brings me to a better place. She asks after the family, and I'm pleased to let her know all's well. I can't say enough about how well she has coped with this. Depression had also been a big problem for her, especially after she lost my dad. But how she's coped is nothing more than tremendous. I'm so proud of her. She is religious, and draws much strength from that, and a good rapport with the minister is welcome. I wish I was that way. I've always wanted a belief, wanting to believe life after death.

I've a trip to the pharmacy today, to collect medication that was missed in my delivery this week. I worry about the amount of medications I'm on. I have tried many times to reduce them, but all attempts have failed. I get ready to go out, checking my phone to make sure they had received my request to leave home. Sure enough they had and I set off. I walk to the pharmacy in the village. On my way, on the other side of the street a man holds up his arm and waves. I acknowledge with a wave. He turns his gaze back to the way he's going. He says nothing, he doesn't have to. He has the mask. It's clear, or as clear as anything is, that there are many of us in contact with V. I see the mask on most trips.

I have to queue at the pharmacy. You can sort of feel the fear in people. A quick glance at the latest addition to the line. Although masked, their frowns give them away. They fidget their feet, hoping not to be noticed they're moving further-away from each other. The line moves quickly, and I'm soon beckoned in. "Name!" Loud enough to do what it's meant to, stops me in my tracks. "Cewell". He moved to the back and rummages through bags of medication. It's the same man who has been there since before Covid. He was then, a friendly talkative man. This is what this hell has done to so many. "Address!!" With that he puts the bag on the counter and moves away. I take it and turn. No thank you, that would mean an opening my mouth again, what a mess. I make haste back to the flat as the rain begins to fall, and glad to close the door, and shut out the world.

I make lunch and a cup of tea, and sit watching the news. A scientist is quizzed about the new strain of Covid. He seems to think that it's somehow changed into a different virus altogether. What kind he didn't know. We're virtually having to go back to the beginning of the virus. It seems that the same science doesn't work on the new one. I wonder for a split second, what would happen if I walked into a police station and told them. Ye!!!, see why it was just a split second?. I've taken as much as I can for the moment and change channel. I'm having a break. It's nice to be normal.

CHAPTER 21.

Within days the death rate grew to horrific levels. Countries reporting as many in one day as they would expect in a month. Fields were taken from farmers to bury the dead. 'Stay Home' was struggling as the army found it difficult to cope, with numbers of them catching the virus. The ones who were still well dressed in fully sealed suits. There's been no word from V. I'm not surprised, he probably knows I'll want to talk numbers. I spend time each day talking to Diane. As you're well aware, I'm not the talkative type. I can talk for

England in my head, but the real thing?. It always sounds right in my head, it's when I open my mouth it all goes wrong.

There's nothing but the virus on tv. The news channel on twenty four hours. The City centre has become a giant hospital. Shops, hotels, buildings now full of Covid patients. The stream of patients mirroring Heathrow arrivals. It's clear the media is being run by governments. They report increased cases, but that is just a fraction of the real number. In the third world, not only are they having to deal with the virus, cholera was now ripping through them. It seems so unfair, V is following our ways, or so it seems, allowing the poor to bear the brunt of this horror. My buzzer sounds. I'm not expecting any delivery. "Who is it?". There's no reply, but I sense there's someone standing outside my door. I take several steps backwards as my heart begins to race. I'm afraid, you would think that by now I would be used to it, but I can't move. I know what I must do, and close my eyes. I manage to sit. There's no need for me to open my eyes. I know that V is with me. "Yes, I am with you Stephen, 'Life' thanks you, and sends you this. Tomorrow you are to come together with others on your wireless networks. I will show you how on your devices. This will begin to tell your leaders to start talking to each other to find a cure for the virus. He has cleared the way for them to do this but you must make them know that they must come together to fight, to live. 'Life' knows how much this is hurting you, and your people, but without this, you will not survive". I ask how we are to do this?. "Just pick up your device and I will let you know".

I still have my eyes closed as the strangeness begins to fade. I open my eyes. V has gone. I walk to my door and open it. Why I need to is pretty stupid. I know he's been, but still need to see the set of footprints. Diane is soon on the phone. "At last, we're going to do something". I agree, and discuss what we think we'll need to do or say. "It's about time. Have you seen those awful pictures?". She refers to online pictures of mass graves in India and Pakistan. Bodies laid out in rows as far as the eyes can see, but we agree that it's good to have something positive at last. There's a beep on my phone that signals a food delivery. Not doing the shopping means less time to see my mam. But she's still good with everything, taking it all in her stride.

I take the rest of the day off, from worry that is. I make myself a sandwich and settle down to some serious tv, Lewis. Yes, I know, sad.

CHAPTER 22.

I wake early. Attempts to get back to sleep fail. It's still dark outside, but I can see frost on the roof of the church opposite, glistening , reflected by the moon. I give it a while before I finally give up at an extra few hours of sleep, and get up. I make myself a drink. I look from the lounge window at cars white over in the street below. The flat is again a tip, but it's not difficult to ignore the mess, and I settle on the sofa and switch on the tv.

V

My thoughts turn to the day ahead, and V's instructions. It seems ages since those first dreams. In reality, although so much has happened, it's only been a short time. I'm hoping that our involvement (at last), will move forward the hunt for a vaccine to end this horror we're in. The news on the tv is as grim as ever. It seems the whole planet is in lockdown. America announces over thirty thousand deaths in one day, more than is usual in a week. It's difficult to accept that this is the only way. It weighs heavily on me. I feel that I'm a part of this, somehow to blame. Really not feeling good at the moment. My thoughts turn to my Mary. I murmur her name, something I do when I get this low, hoping that somehow she'll hear me and put everything right.

I could really do with a walk right now. I'm seriously thinking about it. I put on my coat, but the coward in me takes over and the coat comes off. I spend an hour waking up before getting washed and dressed. It begins to get lighter outside as time moves on. I pick up some rubbish, crisp packets, sweet wrappers. It's a small gesture. I get on line then wish I hadn't. The tv news is usually bad, but this is, well, you know. I take some long hard breaths before I have to move into the kitchen to get away from the horror. I wait in the kitchen until the news moves on to less dire things. It's one o'clock, and I move to the tv controls to switch off the news channel. Before I can, the tv switches off and my iPad lights up. This is it!!!.

I pick it up and see across the top of the screen "Talk to save us. This will be your online page. It is set up and will read that we believe it is vital for all countries of the world come together, to tell governments that they must work together to find a cure for the virus, that is putting our existence in jeopardy. If you agree, please add your name to the list at the bottom of this page. Your name will not be used, only counted". There's an immediate influx of names, and the count flashes up in a blur. "The names you have on your device, are those who have been chosen, like you. You can contact anyone on the list should you wish. This is the first step. Tomorrow it will be in your news and media. I will contact you tomorrow with more information". Names are pouring in, and I get the sense of just how many of us there are. Looking at the list of names, I see Diane at the top. The names have stopped coming in now, there's hundreds of them. Although there's no information about where the people are from, I sense they're local, and expect each town or city to have their own lists. At some point I will probably count just how many there are. I'm a one for statistics.

Mam calls. She's worried after watching the news. I try to tell her that it's going to be ok. She worries about us. I promise that we'll be ok. I move the conversation away from the virus, and she seems less worried as I say goodbye. I could hear another call trying to get me while I was talking to mam. It's as expected, Diane. We're both desperate for the answer to this horror. I tell her about feeling responsible. She understood completely, and tried to help with my thoughts. She's evidently watching the numbers of "Agree's" that are streaming in. She asks if I knew anyone on the list other than her. I told her that I had not really looked through them, but didn't expect to know anyone. The call is cut short by Diane's shopping delivery. It seems all we can do now is wait.

I find myself watching the numbers grow on the web page, from thousands to millions. Undoubtedly V has contacted all the chosen people across the whole world, and to all those with technology have seen the page. There's nothing on the midday news. That seems strange to me, given what I'm seeing on my iPad. There's still that niggle that I may be being used, and V is nothing more than an enemy from another world, that has only the extinction for the human race in mind. I can't dwell too long on that one. Following that thinking can only lead to fear and illness.

I force myself to tidy the flat. If nothing else it will keep my mind, hopefully virus free. It takes me about an hour or so, and I'm pretty physically shattered, but I get a feeling of well being as I look around at my mess free flat. I've always been a bit of a dreamer. I fit so much better in a virtual world. Never felt comfortable inside reality. I suppose I mostly take the easy option with life, rather agreeing, rather than disagreeing, it's so much easier. I hate being hated, having someone think bad of me. It's been a mill stone round my neck all my life. Truth is I want everyone to like me. But of course, not many really care. My phone pings to another message. This is different!!!. A message from the government. I can't remember ever having one of those before. It starts off with the rules of "Stay Home". But as I read on there's a more sinister air to the message.

v

"Being out without permission will be dealt with severely. And then, depending on the situation, and likelihood of transmission of the virus, armed military will take appropriate action, which could include using live ammunition". In other words they've got the ok to kill us again. It's quite a sobering thought, and runs along the lines of nanny states and so on. I can't get my head round the fact that I know this incredible thing, and so called world leaders haven't a clue. Still nothing on the news.

CHAPTER 23.

Evening closes in with still no news. I wonder if governments will actually want to admit to something that is likely to affect their powers. It's common knowledge that they control media coverage. But it can't control the internet, it's worrying there's nothing there either.

Diane and I had our usual daily chat. She's easy to talk to, and is becoming a great friend. We help each other. That alone is so important, it give us something to focus on, away from what we're going through.

My attention is drawn to the time, and the up and coming BBC news. V has the habit of giving us information, then leaving us without news or actions. This is a case in mind. It's not right that there's no news on the net, it doesn't make sense. Still, what does make sense where V is concerned. The nine o'clock news begins with news on the fight for a vaccine. Making progress is mentioned before that warning of severe action for transgressors. Because for the on line news, it's getting difficult for the BBC to deny the real scale of the numbers of deaths. More and more they're having to give out horrific details. Millions are dying each week. Wait!!!. At last. News of the website. "An online website, asking for governments around the world to come together in the fight to produce a vaccine". It goes on to say that the website is being overwhelmed, and that it's world wide. It's great news, a start. V has stated that he'll contact us tomorrow with more information. I really need V to get this sorted. I turn to the decreasing of earth's population. Having to watch millions die, knowing what I do, helpless to do anything. It's all so unbelievable, but I feel I have my hands tied, who's going to listen to the ravings of a handful of people. That's all we need!!!. It seems we have the tail end of hurricane Ray, that hit the east coast of America heading our way. Torrential rain and gale force winds. Mind you, we're not allowed out anyway. Don't know what I'm worried about.

I decide to get something to eat and go to bed. I can't remember what caught my mind, or what I was watching, but sleep got the better of me. Of that I'm glad.

I wake at about half past four, gaze at the tv to see what's happening. I'm really not awake enough to take anything in. I can't get off again, I give it an hour or so before I decide to get up. You've guessed it, coffee. I remember the time when it wasn't, put the kettle on, but get dressed and out to either the local cafe or McDonald's for my coffee. Those were the days. It seems ages since I last listened to the government's do's and don'ts, after all there's a lot more going on to focus the mind. I really don't know how Boris survived as our prime minister. Yes, they have twisted legislation to suit themselves, enabling them to be almost untouchable. But in the early days of the virus, saw him pretty pathetic in his handling of the situation. He actually had the virus himself, and was very poorly for a while. The new regulations are again broadcast. There's nothing new about the website as the daily briefing ends. Looking at the website, I'm amazed at the response. There's that many noughts on the total that I have to check on line what the figures are telling me. It's a stunning two and a half billion. It's less than a day since V had set up the link. I start to feel up lifted about the news. Maybe that's not a particularly good thing, there's still so much that has to done. But I'll enjoy this feeling while it lasted. I call Diane in a better mood than the other day, and after a while I can tell that she's boosted by the way I'm feeling. We are good for each other. When we first met it seemed that I would be constantly talking her down from a worrying, fearful state, but she's actually a really strong person. We give each other a strength, that without the other wouldn't be there. I've spent so much of my life dodging my fears. It's not like my life has been awful, it's not, but it's been a very lonely time since my Mary passed away, and since then I've been fighting to learn to live on my own. I think the fact that I am in some ways coping, tells that I have learnt with time. But I've had to go through some dire times, including that horrible four months in hospital. It's clear that where mental health is concerned, we're still very much in the dark ages. There I go again, focusing on the bad times, idiot!!!.

Lunchtime. I get my usual banana sandwiches and a packet of crisps. My waist tells me that I'm having far too many of the latter. The one o'clock news begins, and this time the lead story is of the increasing numbers signing into the website. There's so many leaving messages. It's at that point my iPad goes blank, it's on charge, so it's not that, and when the tv switches off, I know V is here. The iPad lights up and a message begins to spell out. "'Life' calls on you to enter your cities in a stand we must make to beat this virus. This is what you must do. You must leave your governments no choice but to follow what you are asking. Stephen, in two days, at one o'clock, many thousands will come together in your city to march for humanity. This will happen in every city throughout your world. Do not be afraid Stephen. You and all those who have been vital to save your planet, will be safe. After the marches a vaccine will be found within days, and be available almost immediately after the announcement that one has been found. 'Life' thanks you. He knows how difficult this has been. But because of you, and the people of your world and not its leaders. your world has been given another chance. Your path must be different, it must be in harmony with your planet".

Then!!!. I'm floating in the beauty of the galaxy. It's amazing. "Life' has given this to you. To thank you. Stephen, you can access this at any time. Just close your eyes and think of me".

I know this is the end of this horror. V has gone. 'Life' has completed his mission, and now must move on. I can't be sad. He has left this for me to visit whenever I want. If we throw away this chance that 'Life' has given us, then we do not deserve to carry on.

CHAPTER 24.

It was if the whole world had responded to our call, V's call. There were initial calls from governments around the world against the marches. But the people's word was too powerful. The media was freed from its shackles, and became the people's voice. It was if V had entered into every one of us on the planet. There were no worries, no fear about government warnings. And as the first one o'clock sounded in Tonga. I knew 'Life' and V, had fulfilled their promise. Sure enough the marches all happened. Auckland, Melbourne, Tokyo,

Beijing. As each one o'clock struck, so the marches began. Most moving was the pictures of soldiers laying down their arms to join the marchers in Beijing, with the new leaders of China, applauding on balconies to show their support. And as V had said, within days a new vaccine became available almost immediately. It was announced throughout the world that "A protein, found in blood tests had resulted in the vaccine being developed".

So our world is part of 'Life'. We are all just a cell within 'Life'. Not just a ball of fire that had cooled to such an extent to enable living things to exist, to live in harmony with it. But the life that was so much part of earth, evolved into something that, rather than in harmony, chose to abuse it. Earth began to die, and like anything that would put its existence in jeopardy, it fought back. It infected us with the virus that was benign to itself, but poison to us, which eventually bought us to this.

It's clear that although I have been through this incredible time, there is still so much that we don't understand about 'Life'. Is he the creator?. He talks of his own enemies, and being just a part of something himself. It's mind blowing.

As we watch the gift that 'Life' has given us. I can only hope that we can grasp it, and hold on tightly to it, but deep down I have to admit I fear we won't, and we haven't seen the last of 'Life' and "V".

FOOTNOTE
(from the author)

"V" was born from my need to survive in these difficult times.

With very little knowledge of the written word I was able to lose myself for short times during the days of Covid torment to write this story.

I hope that not only has this novel taken you to a better place for the short time while reading it but also that it shows each and every one of us that we can lose ourselves in passions that we would never have thought possible.

This virus has taken so many lives, touching everyone's life.

I hope that we can learn from our mistakes, so each and every life lost shall not be in vain and our world can become a better place.

Many thanks to my good friend Dinah, without whose help and enthusiasm this novel would never have been completed.

VIRUS